LET THE SEA ROAR

Other Mansk-Svenska publications

Historic Books by G. V. C. Young, OBE

The History of the Isle of Man under The Norse
The Three Legs go to Scandinavia
The Isle of Man and the Faroe Islands —
Two Similar Countries
The Founder of the Bronx

Novels

Rallying Song
by Mona Douglas
My Brother, My King
by Nancy Gaffikin

Children's Books

The Manx Rabbit Family
by Frank Quayle
Illustrated by Nancy Corkish
The Secret of Black Dog Cave
by Eve Jennings

LET THE SEA ROAR

by

Ethel Harper

The Mansk-Svenska Publishing Co. Ltd.,
Peel, Isle of Man

DEDICATION

To Jonathan, April, Philippa and John

ACKNOWLEDGEMENTS

I would like to express my sincere thanks to the very many people who have assisted me in my research work and, in particular, to **Mona Firth** and **Freda Dennis** of Castletown who gave me complete access to their wonderful library, and to the staff of the Manx Museum for their help and kindness.

I would like to thank **George Quayle** of Lezayre who at one time farmed "Ellanbane" and gave me invaluable information which enabled me to get the true atmosphere of Ellanbane and the surrounding country.

ISBN 0 9077 15 15 X Hardback
ISBN 0 9077 15 16 8 Paperback

Published by Mansk-Svenska Publishing Company Limited.
Typeset in Photon Times by Keyspools (IOM) Ltd.,
Second Avenue, Onchan, Isle of Man
Printed by The Leinster Leader Limited, Naas, Co. Kildare, Republic of Ireland.

CHAPTER ONE

They say that coming events cast their shadows before: be that as it may, I still have poignant memories of a certain late autumn evening in 1596.

Here we were, my father, Huan Standish, and I Myles, his only son, walking together along the Lezayre road near Ramsey in the north of the Isle of Man. We were returning home from a visit to my aunt's house in Sulby; a neighbouring hamlet.

My father was taking long steady strides, his great hand holding my small one firmly, while I trotted along beside him almost out of breath in a desperate effort to keep up with him.

Daylight was fading, candles were being lit in upland farmsteads, tiny points of light, glowing, warm and luminous, against the blackness of the hills. Already there was a touch of frost in the air, tingling my ears, and setting the first stars shimmering, and trembling, above the dark outline of the Nappin Ridge.

We had been travelling along for some time in complete silence. My father was ever a quiet pre-occupied man, and I never felt wholly at ease in his company, finding conversation with him difficult: yet at the same time I admired him, and loved him dearly.

Suddenly, without altering pace, he bent his head and looked steadily into my eyes for a moment or two. Then, gazing away into the distance as if searching for words, he began to speak of my mother who had died at my birth.

Surprised and vaguely uneasy, I looked quickly up at him. Never before had he spoken of her to me.

"I wish your mother had lived, Myles," he was saying in a slow quiet voice, as if to impress his words on my mind. "For even after so long a time I am still desolate without her. All joy went out of my life when she died."

He spoke brokenly, and was silent for a few moments. Then he added "You must always be honourable and trustworthy as she would have wished, my son:" his voice still full of distress.

"Yes Father, I will be good, of course I will" I answered, moved with a quick pity, and an earnest desire to please him.

As I continued to gaze up at him, his whole expression became sombre, and I was dismayed to see a slight trembling about his mouth, and the glint of tears on his cheeks.

Young as I was, barely past my twelfth birthday, I realised a little of his

5

darkness of soul and, struggling in vain to find words of comfort, I squeezed his hand in a gesture of sympathy.

We continued along the road in silence again. A weight of melancholy hung between us and it was a relief to turn at last into the avenue of splendid trees which lead to the manor house of Ellanbane, our home in Lezayre.

As soon as we arrived at the sweeping semi-circular driveway in front of the house, I stopped short, looked up at him with an uncomfortable smile and wriggled my hand free from his grasp. "I will see you tonight at supper, Father," I said and, without waiting for a reply, rushed on through the half open front door, across the wide flagged hall and down a short flight of steps into the kitchen beyond.

It was always warm and comforting in there, full of the sweet natural smells of home: of baking bread, turf fires and good dinners.

A big fire was blazing away in the hearth and a cluster of rushlight candles on the chimney piece filled the room with a snug glow but, best of all, Kitty our housekeeper was there: Kitty with her laughing blue eyes and rosy cheeks, who loved me and looked after me with all the carefulness of a good mother.

She kissed me as I scampered in, removed my topcoat and hat and hung them on a hook behind the kitchen door asking "Did you enjoy your visit to Sulby?", quite sure that I had. I nodded vigorously, and felt happy to be home again.

She poured out a cup of milk for me from a jug standing on a round scrubbed table in the centre of the room, and I went to sit and drink it on my customary seat, a stone bench built deep within the open fireplace, while Kitty and a small platoon of housemaids busied themselves with preparations for supper.

I had not been sitting there long, when there was a clatter of hobnailed boots on the cobbled yard outside and, a little later, the sound of the scullery door swinging open with a jolt. Then George Quayle, Kitty's sweetheart, came in, bidding us a brisk "Good Everin" as he entered. George was one of our tenant farmers, a large handsome fellow, with strong shoulders and powerful hands. As usual, he came and dropped onto the bench beside me, giving me a comradely smile and stretching his legs to the fire.

He was a talkative fellow, a great teller of tales, and soon had me chuckling at his droll anecdotes, which he told well, building them up gradually with humorous exaggerations to an absurd climax, and now, getting well into his stride, he launched into a story about a young friend of his, a parson from Ballabeg in the south of the Island.

"I met him in Derby Haven the other day", he began, "when he had just returned from England. He had been over there to offer himself as candidate for a living that had become vacant in a richly endowed country parish. He had been a little dismayed, however, to learn that a classical scholar was desired, one who could introduce a little Latin or Greek into the Sunday discourses. The deacon and members considered this would add lustre to the standing of their church in the county. Alas, my friend had neither", said George, "but", and here he gave me a meaningful nudge, "he is a very cunning fellow and, when he discovered that the congregation was composed mainly of farming families, who knew no other language but English, he larded the sermon he was invited to preach with scraps of Manx Gaelic. 'Notice the clarity of this scripture in the original Greek' he cried in the middle of his homily, and gave them a sentence or two in Manx. Then, a little later, 'See how precise is the Latin text', adding a little more in his mother tongue.

"The congregation was so impressed with his learning that he was given the rectorship right away. And so," George went on, "he has come back to the Island to pack his belongings, and bid his friends goodbye, before taking over the parish." George ended the story roaring with laughter, and I was holding my sides at this account of his friend's craftiness.

To what extent his yarns were meant to be believed, I never really knew, but they were always amusing and it was pleasant to listen to them as we sat friendly and easy together by the fire. He had just embarked upon another saga when Kitty interrupted him in mid-sentence to tell me it was time to go in to supper. She poured some water into a jug from a kettle slung on a hook over the fire and, leaving friend George sitting contentedly in the chimney corner, I carried it into the scullery, washed my hands and face and set myself to rights, and went back up the steps and along the hall to the dining room at the front of the house.

It was a large elegant room, dark panelled, full of massive family portraits and richly carved furniture. My father, in company with my grandfather, the head of our household, was already seated at the far end of a long candle-lit table. I took my place between them, and my grandfather, inclining his head towards me with a brief smile, rang a silver hand-bell for supper to be brought in. He was an erect, spare-framed man, with alert blue eyes and full silver beard. In his movements he was vigorous and agile, yet, although at that time he was not quite fifty years, to my young eyes he appeared immensely old. He rarely took much notice of me except to scold if I fidgeted or spilled anything on the tablecloth. All the same I had a genuine affection for him, albeit mixed with not a little fear.

All through the meal, my father and he discussed day to day estate matters, and there was a curious accord between them as they rambled on about schemes for draining some low lying meadowland, and the repairing of several farm buildings. They grumbled a good deal too about the poor corn harvest and the scandalously low price secured for beef cattle at Sulby mart the previous week. They were both full of ideas for improving their land and stock, and I kept glancing from one to the other marvelling at their enthusiasm, while I was altogether lost in boredom. Nevertheless, it was good to see my father in better spirits even though he seemed tired. There were purple smudges beneath his eyes, and his face was pale and drawn.

After supper we moved into the drawing room, where a fire, piled high with logs, leaped and crackled in a cheerful blaze. My father's sheep dog, Scamp, was stretched before it, feigning sleep, but with one eye slightly open, and his tail thumping a welcome as we came through the door. A chess table was drawn to one side of the hearth, with the pieces set out ready for play. On it was also a decanter of wine and two glasses.

It was a quiet room, beautifully proportioned and full of soft peaceful shadows. Candles in several wall sconces burnt clear and warm as the two men poured out a glass of wine apiece, then drew up a couple of high-backed chairs to the table and commenced their game. I got down on the hearthrug beside Scamp, whom I adored, fondling him, rubbing his ears and stroking him. I was hoping my presence would be forgotten, and I would be able to stay up late, but I was unlucky, for in a very short time my father twisted in his chair and caught my eye.

"Time for bed, son," he said with a half smile. Reluctantly, I said "Goodnight", and kissed them both. Taking a lighted candle from amongst a group on the high mantelpiece, I went up to my room.

I stayed awake for a long time that night, comfortable between sheets made cosy from a recent application of the warming pan. The curtains were undrawn, and I lay watching the branches of the tall trees before my windows, moving gently against a starry sky. I was thinking about my mother, trying to picture her face and wishing she had not died, thus leaving my father so sad.

When at last I did fall asleep it was not for long. I was awakened before dawn by the sound of a great confusion of footsteps thudding to and fro in my father's room directly below mine. There was a constant murmuring of voices, and the air seemed full of urgency. I sat up in bed and listened for a moment or two, then, seized by a feeling of apprehension, got out, threw on my dressing gown and ran downstairs. I found my grandfather and Kitty standing, ashen faced, on the landing outside my father's room, and I listened, horror-stricken, as Kitty, holding me close, and smoothing the hair across my forehead, said "Your father, Myles, had a seizure in the early hours of the morning. He is dead!"

CHAPTER TWO

My father's funeral took place three days later, on an overcast morning of lowering clouds and squally rain-laden winds.

From first light, the passing bell at Lezayre church had tolled with a solemn clangour. Then, at the appointed hour, my grief-stricken grandfather and I headed the slowly moving procession behind the coffin to our private chapel near the house. After us my aunt, my father's widowed sister, walked with Fernando, the fifth Earl of Derby, a kinsman. Then followed the Island's legislature and all twenty-four members of the House of Keys, with whom my father had served as Speaker. Finally, came Kitty and the rest of the household, including tenants and workers from our several farms.

The service, conducted by the Bishop, was full of ceremonial, and almost incomprehensible to me, but the majestic language was very moving, and I followed the words in the prayer book with bowed head and quivering heart.

Later, at the graveside, as the coffin was lowered into the oblong of freshly dug earth, I was sick with misery. Hot tears rolled down my cheeks, and it was at that precise moment that I turned my back upon God. I was furiously angry with Him for allowing my father to die. He could not, I reasoned, be the kind heavenly Father I had been taught to believe He was, and from then onwards I stopped saying my prayers.

The weeks that followed were intolerable. They had the quality of a bad dream. The melancholy of death had cast an unfamiliar light over everything and nothing seemed real anymore. Then, slowly, the current of life returned and, although the loss of my father still hurt, I left off crying myself to sleep at nights, and I began to feel that in time I might be happy again.

My grandfather, stoically trying to hide his distress, put on a front of cheerfulness and began to invite neighbouring families of substance to dine with us. With plenty of company around, he found it less easy to brood: nevertheless, he often looked forlorn and sad, and I worried about him.

He treated me now with greater intimacy, and there was much more affection between us. He had decided, he told me, that it was time I had a formal education. Prior to his death my father had taught me my letters, but my curriculum had been somewhat erratic, depending on the time he could spare from running the estate. Now, however, arrangements were made for the Rev. William Crowe, a man much thought of for his scholarship, to take me in hand. So every morning I

9

went to his house in the parish of Jurby where, besides Latin, a subject which he considered most essential, he gave me a good grounding in mathematics, French and English.

Then each afternoon, with Scamp, who had now adopted me, following close at my heels, I hurried over to "Glentrammon", George Quayle's farm, a quiet place, where I felt happy and secure. George was especially kind to me these days. He wanted me to forget my troubles, to be happy again, and we became almost like father and son.

Now that the harvest was over, and the fields calm with the approach of winter, he had time to spare from the work of the farm, and we went rambling about the countryside. Most days we walked together, through deep, narrow lanes, bounded by brambles and hawthorn, to the upper reaches of the lovely Glen Auldyn, or climbed "Glen Trammon Tops", but best of all I enjoyed exploring the flat mysterious country of the "Ayres" where George taught me to distinguish the various call notes of birds, and to name every wild flower we saw.

It was a delight to roam the countryside with George: for me they were steps into enchanted places. He was an ardent naturalist for whom no bird or beast or growing thing lacked beauty. He taught me to love the earth and its cycles, seed-time and harvest, sowings and reapings, the loveliness of woodland and meadow, the brooding mysteries of solitary places. Then all too soon our excursions were suspended. Mellow autumn ended abruptly in a bout of wild stormy weather. Sheep were brought in from hill pastures: Scamp bounding before us up the steep inclines, scenting the flock, then turning them neatly to drive them down into their winter quarters.

Before long, Christmas was close upon us and Kitty did her best to bring an air of good cheer into the house. From the beginning of December, our kitchen was full of the delicious spicy smell of festive cooking. Mincepies and bunloaves filled the fireside oven and, as the great day drew near, geese and turkeys, plucked and stuffed ready for roasting, occupied several long shelves in the pantry. In an iron cauldron, slung over the fire on a showrie, plum puddings tumbled and bobbed about for hours on end. Sprigs of holly, bright with shining red berries, were tucked behind pictures and boughs of evergreen hung in fine bunches from ceilings and walls.

Traditionally, on Christmas Eve, the house was thrown open to all who cared to call, and this year was no exception. The church choir arrived to sing old Manx carvels, and the "white boys" came to perform their ancient farce, all foregathering later in the kitchen to enjoy Kitty's mincepies and home-brewed beer. On that night, the whole place was once again full of laughter and jollity.

My grandfather performed his duties affably enough, welcoming all visitors, making sure that everyone was well-fortified with meat and drink and distributing gifts of money to the household staff, but later, when everyone had departed, and the house quiet again, and I wished him a "Happy Christmas", he did not reply for a moment or two. Then, gazing at me wistfully, he said "Your father, Myles, was still with us last year," and the hopeless feeling of irretrievable loss came

10

flooding back to both of us.

Christmas Day, however, brought, as usual, it's own particular magic. There had been a fall of snow during the night and, when I awoke, my room seemed strangely light. Gazing out of the window, as I washed and dressed, the whole earth, as far as I could see, was blanketed in sparkling whiteness. All sounds were muted, the surrounding fields quiet and still, and I could only faintly hear the footsteps of a cowman as he passed beneath my window with a brimming bucket of milk for the kitchen.

After a substantial breakfast, and warmly wrapped against the cold, my grandfather and I set off for Church, he mounted on a big chestnut mare and I sitting pillion behind him. The air was crisp and exhilarating as we rode together in companionable silence. Shafts of early morning sun gleamed from a pale blue sky, dazzling the eyes and touching far off snow-capped hills with barrets of gold. Across velvety white fields a sound of distant chimes came ringing, sweet and silvery in the frosty air. Truly, on a morning like this it was impossible to be downcast for long.

Turning into the Lezayre road we overtook many happy little family groups, all, like us, on their way to sing carols and rejoice on this, the Lord's birthday. They were full of an air of suppressed excitement, and there was a lively clatter of talk as they plunged along in the powdery snow, leaving a track of ankle-deep footprints behind them as they went.

Just for a moment, I caught their enthusiasm. In spite of my doubts and rebellion against God, I was overwhelmed with the mystery and wonder of Christmas and later, when we were assembled together in Church, I joined in singing the lovely haunting melodies as heartily as any there. When we returned home, it was to an excellent meal for, on this one day in all the year, dinner was served soon after midday, and our friends, the Quayles from Ballaskelly and the Cannells from Michael, had been invited to share the feast with us. It began with a fine roast turkey, flanked by a brace of plump ducklings, and followed by a baron of beef and collops of pork, all washed down with plenty of home-brewed ale. The maids bustled about, handing round vegetables and sauces and replenishing empty dishes with full ones, until at last the great round plum pudding was brought in, lit up and covered in a blue flame. When this had been eaten and praised, the company moved into the drawing room, where they sat at ease before a crackling log fire, exchanging anecdotes and passing round bowls of nuts and sweetmeats, which they ate with a drowsy pleasure.

I sat with them for a while, then slipped away unobtrusively and, taking Scamp with me, went over to spend the rest of the day with George Quayle, Scamp bounding ahead along the frozen lanes, barking with excitement and looking over his shoulder now and then to make sure I was still in view. I found George in the warm, milky-smelling cowhouse. He was leaning almost motionless against a stall, surveying a roan heifer that had had some difficulty in calving. When he saw me, he jerked his head in greeting and I went and stood quietly beside him, following his gaze.

He stood for some time without shifting, looking down at the poor beast with a helpless, uncertain air. Then he began speaking soothing words of encouragement to her. His voice was full of persuasion, and after a while, to our great relief, she slowly raised herself to her feet and, lowing softly, began to chew the cud. He gave her a forkful or two of hay and then, with the utmost gentleness, drew her newly-born calf from a dark corner of the stall, and put him to his mother. She turned her head and licked the little fellow, as with great concentration he began to suck. George turned to me and chuckled, his face alight with satisfaction.

"Mother and son both doing well" I said. "And on Christmas Day too", he replied, as he gave me a triumphant slap on the back. We smiled happily at each other, feeling we had just witnessed a minor miracle. By now the afternoon was closing in and George was obliged to milk and fodder the stock by lantern light. I helped by feeding the hogs and poultry, and carried several foaming buckets of milk across the yard to the dairy.

We strained the milk into pans and put it away, washed our hands at a pump in the yard and dried them on a piece of clean sacking tied over the pump-head, then made our way into the square stone flagged farm kitchen.

Betsey Mylecraine, George's aunt, was busy stoking up the already glowing fire with turves, shovelling them high up into the chimney, and the strange aromatic smell they gave out held a fragrance almost like incense. A lantern, hanging from the ceiling, shed a soft light on a scrubbed deal table in the centre of the room, and from a pot hanging above the fire came a delicious smell of broth.

Betsey turned from the fire and surveyed us crossly. "What kept you?" she cried. "Jane Corlett is near her time and I should have been with her an hour since." George explained about the heifer and, slightly mollified, she ladled out some broth into two bowls and put them on the table, together with a couple of horn spoons. Then she fished out a large bone from the pot for Scamp, who wagged his feathery tail and took it into a corner behind the turf basket to enjoy.

As we sat up to the table, Betsey took a long homespun cloak from a hook behind the door and drew it closely about her. She was a tall, gaunt woman, grey haired and sallow, with darting, heavily lidded, black eyes that missed nothing. Since George's parents had died years ago, she had kept house for him and was also the local handy-woman, helping at every birth and death for miles around. She lived within reach in a small cottage belonging to the farm. Before she left for Jane Corlett's house, she came over and laid a thin, veined hand on George's arm. "My brother wants you to go to his house to-night to do 'a bit of writing' for him" she said, bending her head and looking earnestly into his face. George raised an eyebrow and glanced sharply up at her.

"Is Uncle Caesar unwell then?" he asked, for, to the Manx born, doing 'a bit of writing' always means to draw up a will.

Betsey shook her head. "He is well enough" she replied. Then, leaning gravely towards him, "He has a very good reason for wanting to set his affairs in order, very good indeed. Please do as he asks".

Slipping me a sidelong look, she pursed her lips and, glancing back at George, said "I expect my brother would prefer to see you alone."

"I hope he would not" said George: "anything he wants to say I am sure he will not mind saying in front of Myles – the boy is the soul of descretion."

Betsey did not speak again but, shrugging her shoulders, stalked away through the door, obviously resenting my presence.

So later, when we had finished eating, we buttoned on our greatcoats and, leaving Scamp stretched out before the fire until our return, we set off into the cold night for a two mile walk along the Jurby road. On the ground the snow was unmarred. A full moon was riding high in a clear starry sky, and Caesar Mylecraine's farmstead, set on a rise with a copse of trees behind it, stood out in sharp relief. It was a comfortable, prosperous-looking place, with almost the appearance of a small manor house.

George knocked on the front door and, when Voirrey, Caesar's daughter, opened it and recognised us, her voice was warm and full of welcome. "Come in, come in" she said, and led the way into a cosy living room, well-lit with plenty of candles. "George and Myles are here, Father," she announced cheerfully.

Her father was sitting facing the chimney place. A low table before him held an assortment of articles, a writing block, an ink horn, a box of quills and a sand caster. He was a man of about seventy years, small, wispy and shrivelled, with a long nose and shrewd grey eyes set rather too closely together. He had the reputation of being extremely careful with his money, and I had often heard him referred to as "a miser", but he had always treated me with great friendliness on the few occasions I had visited him with George, and I liked him.

As we entered he sprang up, and pumped our hands vigorously. "Thank you both for coming so soon", he said: "this small piece of business will not take long." We loosened our greatcoats, and he disposed us on an oak settle drawn at right angles to the fire, and within easy reach of the writing materials.

Voirrey took a couple of candles from a wall sconce and set them in the middle of the table. She was a striking young woman, just twenty years old, not pretty but tall and well built, with auburn curls swept on top of her head and tied with a green ribbon.

She stood for a moment looking down at her father, bright-eyed and a little embarrassed. "I am going out for a while, Father," she said. Then, flashing a sweeping smile at George and me, "please excuse me" she added.

Mylecraine, head thrown back, contemplated her gloomily. "Not to meet that foreign rascal I hope?" A grimace, and a twitch of her shoulders, was her only reply to that as she turned and walked to the door with a sturdy grace.

When she had closed it behind her, George sat back on the settle, arms folded across his chest. "Well, Uncle", he said, "shall we get down to business?" The old man cleared his throat, then leaned across the table and tapped my arm. "Be sure and attend to your lessons, Myles," he said, "for, as you can see, I am unable to read or write, and I find it a great handicap, especially at a time like this." Then, looking at George, he began on a long preamble.

"I have decided to make a new will" he said. "I have been driven to do this

13

since Voirrey seems bent on marrying a man I detest. In a previous will drawn up many years ago, I left everything I possessed to her with no strings attached, but now I feel I must make it a condition that she takes a suitable husband, one who is honest and hardworking. This fellow is only after her for her money: of that I am convinced. Voirrey is a good girl but headstrong and wilful. She says she is not interested in how I leave the bulk of my money, but is asking me to give her a dowry now so that she can marry this fellow. However, I have made up my mind – she shall not have a penny piece of mine, either now or ever, if she persists in this foolishness. I shall leave everything to my sister Betsey." He leaned back scowling, thin lips compressed into a straight line, eyes sparking with indignation.

George was regarding him thoughtfully. "Who is this man, and why are you so against him marrying Voirrey?" he asked.

"He is a ne'er do well Frenchman, a survivor from a ship wrecked near the Point of Ayre. He lives meagrely, doing odd jobs around the farms – a drunkard and a great womaniser, they tell me – but Voirrey will not hear a word said against him. I love her dearly and I want her to be happy, but I am taking the only course open to me. I am hoping that, when this fellow learns she has neither money nor prospects, he will leave her alone." He fell silent for a moment or two, then suddenly broke out again, his voice gentle and tender now: "I must protect her, surely you can see that George? Her dead mother would have wished me to do so."

George did not press him further. He drew the writing-block towards him, dipped quill in ink and scratched away to his uncle's dictation. Within ten minutes the document was completed. He sanded it and handed it to his uncle who, after he had made his mark, folded it and put it carefully into his pocket. Two of his friends, a doctor and a Ramsey businessman, would sign it for him he said. Then, pushing back the table, he came and sat beside us on the settle.

George twisted round and gave him an affectionate, teasing look. "Do you know, Uncle," he said, "before to-night I had no idea you were so rich. Farming must be very prosperous in your part of the country."

Mylecraine gave a boisterous laugh. "It did not all come from farming", he declared, "but mostly by way of an amazing stroke of luck. If I tell you how it came about, I need hardly say that you are not to speak of it to any other person." George and I assured him of our discretion, and the old man sat back full of self-satisfaction and regaled us with a most amazing story.

"About ten years ago", he said, "there was a terribly stormy night. It happened in the middle of August just as the corn was ready for cutting."

Here George broke in: "I remember it well," he said, "the crops were nearly all ruined, and many fields were turned into quagmires. A most disastrous harvest time it was, the worst I can ever recall."

Mylecraine nodded and went on. "Well, the following morning, I got up early and took a walk over my land to see what damage had been done to the crops and stock. I was in for a shock. My farm, as you know, is divided by the River Llen and, during the storm, there had been a cloudburst. The river had overflowed

14

its banks, and boulders and uprooted trees lay scattered in all directions. I stood for a while gazing at the devastation with a heavy heart when, all at once, I spotted a dark object bobbing about in the middle of the river and travelling swiftly downstream. Without stopping to think, I waded in, up to my knees, over the churning torrent and grabbed it. It was with great difficulty that I pulled it to the bank, straining and heaving with all my might. It turned out to be an oak trunk, so heavy that I doubt I could have managed it by myself had not the strong current helped to carry it in my direction.

"Eventually I drew it clear of the water and, as the wood was rotten, I was able to prise the lid open quite easily with my jack knife and it came away leaving a solid brass lock intact. I was astounded and quite overcome to find the trunk filled up to the brim with gold sovereigns. Lying on top of all, was a beautiful silver cross.

"After filling my pockets, I shut the lid and covered the trunk with brushwood and gorse bawns, then returned home for some sacks in which to carry the rest of the booty. So you see," he said, "far from being a moderately successful farmer, I am now a very rich man."

There was a long silence as George eyed him speculatively. "Did you never try to discover to whom it belonged?" he asked eventually.

"No" replied his uncle: "it is my belief that it had been buried near the river by some thieving smuggler, and washed down into it when the banks caved in. So I feel no guilt about sticking to it."

George frowned in disapproval, but he was a tactful man and said no more on the subject. However, I was inclined to agree with his uncle that, on this occasion, findings were keepings. The whole story intrigued me and, overcome with curiosity, I smiled at Mylecraine and asked "What did you do with the silver cross?" "Ah", he said, "I still have it. You must see it." He got up and went over to a corner near the door where stood a little oak pedestal table, and on it a small shagreen box. He bent over and fiddled about for a few seconds, and when he came back he was carrying the cross, flat on the palm of his hand. He laid it carefully on the table in front of us, and it gleamed softly in the candlelight.

"It is a lovely thing" said Mylecraine, and we both agreed it was indeed very beautiful. After we had examined it and admired it, he put it away in its box almost with reverence. I was not to see it again until many years later and in the most unusual circumstances.

15

CHAPTER THREE

Spring came early that year and George, with only one hired man to help him, was hard at work from early morning to sunset planting corn and barley in his fields. He also had a crop of spring lambs to attend to and often had to leave his bed in the small hours to help at the birthing. Then, providentially, a good rainfall had soaked the earth, and the dun coloured fields were soon sprouting a misty green growth, giving promise of an abundant harvest, and making the long hours and laborious work seem well worthwhile.

During all this busy time he had not come so often to see Kitty but, when the pressure of work eased off a little, he once more appeared each evening. Kitty, however, was often edgy and short-tempered with him, even though he was invariably kind and gentle towards her. It was quite some time before he found out what was bothering her.

One night, as he and I were sitting cosily together in the ingle-nook, he was holding forth with great satisfaction about how well his crops were coming along, and what a good lambing time it had been. Kitty, who was bustling about the kitchen, washing dishes and sweeping the floor, and had so far paid no attention to him, now broke in, her voice high-pitched and vexed.

"I am glad", she said, "that your affairs are going so well for you, but I wish you would consider me a little more. I wanted you to take me to Maughold fair last week but, of course, you were too busy and I had to go alone! You were missing too when I went to the 'Laa Columb Killey'. Perhaps I should look for a man who would put me first sometimes, someone who would not take me so much for granted. I am sick and tired of your cows and sheep and barley. You think more of them than you do of me. I am quite sure of that."

George, who was not easily put out, sat glaring at her, his face frowning and sombre. When at last she paused for breath, he got up from his seat and walked, heavy-shouldered, and awkwardly, towards her. He caught and held her wrist. "Is that all you have to say?" he asked.

Kitty pulled her wrist from his grasp, and shrugged her shoulders. "Yes", she said wryly, "I think that puts things straight between us."

George looked appealingly at her for a moment or two. Then he said: "I am sorry you feel I have neglected you, but I had hoped you would understand how hard I must work in the Springtime of the year. The farm is just beginning to pay after many lean years, and this success has only come after a lot of hard work. I

16

was too tired to come to see you when my work was finished. I have no better excuse to offer, and if you wish to look for someone more suitable for a husband, then there is nothing further to be said."

There was a long silence as they gazed at one another with aggressive eyes, then George turned away and stormed off, heavy-footed, through the door.

I was shocked. I had never before heard them speak unkindly to one another but now it looked as if all was over between them. Kitty held back her tears until the sound of his footsteps crossing the yard outside had died away. Then she sat down heavily on a stool before the fire and wept. I tried to comfort her but without success, and for the next few days she went about very quiet and dejected.

During the months that followed, George sent no message to her nor spoke her name to me. He was a proud man, and Kitty's outburst had hurt him deeply.

But Kitty was not left desolate for long. Quite soon another young man appeared on the scene – a swarthy young Frenchman named Jacques. He was handsome in a flashy sort of way, slimly built, tallish, with smooth black hair and bold arrogant black eyes.

He treated me in a half patronising way, and I took a great dislike to him. It was easy to guess that he was the same fellow that had been courting Voirrey Mylecraine, for foreigners are scarce in our part of the world.

I talked it over with George, and he admitted that he was aware of this turn of events. He smiled at me a little ruefully. "I have been much at fault over this affair, Myles," he said: "I was very blind. I should have seen Kitty's point of view and tried to spend a little more time with her or, at the very least, discussed my problems with her. I have since realised that I did take it for granted that she would understand how things were with me, and so I have only myself to blame for the quarrel. However," he went on, "in spite of everything, I am inclined to think things will come right for us in the end. This fellow Jacques is, I hear, a great philanderer. He has courted almost every girl in the district, but never for very long. So I am awaiting my chance, and when he moves on to fresh pastures, as I hope he will, I will go to Kitty and eat humble pie. Somehow I think she will forgive me."

George was right, for after a time Jacques came no more, and one afternoon, about a year later, as I was setting off for Glentrammon, Kitty called me to her. "Tell George", she said, looking a little sheepish, "I have had enough of Jacques – it is all over and done with and I am sorry I have been such a fool."

When I gave George her message he was overjoyed. "Thank God" was his only remark as he went off, hotfoot, to see her.

All bitterness was soon swept away between them, and an early date was set for their wedding. So now my grandfather was faced with the task of finding a new housekeeper at fairly short notice.

He wrote immediately to Mrs Isabella Standish, one time of Standish Hall in Lancashire and now living in Ormskirk, asking if she would be willing to come and run the household for him. She was the widow of a distant cousin of my grandfather, and had been left in straitened circumstances with a young son and daughter of her own to rear, as well as her husband's daughter from a previous marriage: this had been to a widow with a little girl whom he had brought up as his own and to whom he had given his name.

Mrs Standish's reply came quickly: "Your offer is a godsend", she wrote, "and I shall be pleased to come."

By early summer she arrived, together with her little family, and I stood in the hall with my grandfather to receive them. Rose, Mrs Standish's daughter, just seven years old, was a pretty, delicately-formed child with golden curls, and a pair of lively blue eyes. Her step-daughter, Barbara, about my own age, was tall, auburn-haired and handsome, rather than pretty. Both girls I found most amiable and friendly but William, their brother, I did not care for. He was three years younger than I but very much taller. He had a round plump face and treacle-brown eyes, drawn down at the corners, giving him an artful, sly expression. It was not a pleasant face. As we shook hands, he gave a loud, irritating laugh.

"My word," he said, as he looked me over from head to toe in an exaggerated fashion, "You are small. I can just barely see you!" Everyone, my grandfather included, laughed at this rude remark, but I was angry.

Stiffly, I told him that being small does not count for as much as people think. "I intend", I said haughtily, "to make as much success in life as those twice my size."

"Oh really", he replied with a malicious grin, "but you will have to try very hard indeed to equal the exploits of a big fellow like me." So saying, he snapped his fingers disdainfully in my face and went off with my grandfather to the stables, to become acquainted with a piebald gelding which had been placed at his disposal.

Mrs Standish, whom I was henceforth to call Aunt Bella, was a woman of about forty-five, slim, dark and elegant, and bristling with energy. Within a week she had engaged a governess for the two girls, and persuaded my grandfather to enrol William and me at the Academic School at Castletown.

Hence the whole tenor of my life was very quickly changed. George and Kitty were married, and happily settled at Glentrammon. Ellanbane was no longer the peaceful, homelike place I loved, and now it seemed certain that self-satisfied and conceited Cousin William was henceforth to be my constant companion. I did not relish the thought!

Aunt Bella had arranged that we were to lodge at "Knockrushen" with a Mr and Mrs Christian, friends of my grandfather, returning only at holiday time to Ellanbane. So, on the evening before leaving for Castletown, I took Scamp to stay with George and Kitty. I was sad at heart to leave him, but I knew he would have a good home with them and be kindly treated.

Then, early next morning, when the first shafts of sun were gilding the sky, and the air full of a fresh smell of dew on grass, we set off, William mounted on the piebald gelding and me on my own bay mare, our belongings packed in bulky rolls and strapped behind our saddles. For the first mile or so we hardly spoke. I was full of resentment against William, for ever since our first meeting he had constantly twitted me about my lack of inches, and also lately had begun to make fun of my red hair. This latter had aggravated me a great deal for I had always been rather proud of my flaming thatch. But, thinking things over as we rode along, I came to the conclusion it would be better for all concerned if we tried to get along together. It would be difficult if unpleasantness persisted between us while living under the same roof, and with family friends to boot.

I told him what was in my mind, but with the proviso that I was quite prepared to stay at loggerheads if that was what he wanted. Oddly enough, he agreed at once to be friends, and became inordinately agreeable, almost mealy-mouthed. But this only made me suspicious of his real intentions. He was much too plausible for my liking.

At Peel we stopped at a small hostelry, where we foddered and watered the horses and also had an excellent meal ourselves. Early afternoon found us at Castletown.

CHAPTER FOUR

We rode at a gentle trot down Malew Street, the main thoroughfare of the little town, a higgledy-piggledy street where fine houses of the gentry were mixed up together with labourers' tumbledown dwellings. There were also a few shops, a smithy and a small tavern where we were to stable our horses.

Coming away from the stable yard, we had only a short distance to walk to the market square. We found this a very busy place, for to-day was a market day and people from all over the Island had assembled there both to buy and to sell all manner of goods.

Beneath the ramparts of the great limestone castle, booths were set up full of farm produce, some piled high with vegetables, others with pats of yellow butter, little round cheeses, baskets of eggs and flitches of bacon. Others displayed bonnags and soda cakes, pots of jam and jellies, as well as Manx knobs and jujubes, peppermint sticks and pink and white sugar mice. Apple-cheeked farmers' wives in voluminous holland aprons and pretty flowered sun-bonnets were crying their wares at the top of their voices.

Housewives with laden baskets over their arms, farmers with their dogs and fishermen in clumsy sea boots and reeky oilskins were chatting together in little groups. Hordes of children were running in and out between the booths playing tip-cat, and shrieking with merriment. Everyone seemed full of good humour and enjoyment.

Just as we were threading our way through the crowds, one of the children, being hotly pursued by a companion, darted directly in front of William, causing him to stumble. William immediately seized him by the sleeve and cuffed his ear. "Plague take you, lad," he yelled, then cuffed the other ear even more violently.

"William, stop, you fool," I exclaimed, and grabbed hold of his arm before he could do more serious damage.

The child began to howl with anguish, whereupon a sturdy farmer's wife, with the light of battle in her eye, left her stall and came running to his aid. Shaking her fist in William's face, she stormed and raved at him. "How dare you lay hands on my son" she cried: "I will have the law on you, you young whipper snapper." Her voice, loud and penetrating, brought a gang of youths flocking round to see what was to do. They encircled us closely, thus blocking our way and looking, I thought, quite rough and menacing.

William eyed the woman in embarrassed silence as on she ranted. Then, drawing some money from his pocket, he offered it to her. She snatched it with alacrity but, as she returned to her stall, taking with her the howling child, she was still calling down curses on William's head, and her eyes were blazing with fury. The crowd of youths, seeing all hope of a row developing fade away, quickly dispersed, and we were able to continue on our way unmolested.

We crossed the square, turned into Queen Street then along the Scarlett Road. Slipping William a sidelong glance as we went, I said "It was fortunate for us that you were able to get rid of that woman so easily. Those fellows looked ugly customers to me and were obviously spoiling for a fight." William, with lip thrust out and a face like thunder, did not reply and, save to mutter a few fluent oaths under his breath, did not trouble to speak again until we arrived at Knockrushen. He felt he had been made to look small, and clearly resented it.

Knockrushen, we discovered, was the only house on the Scarlett Road, and almost completely hidden by trees. Stone built and impressive, it stood well back on a slight eminence, sheltered by a high wall and overlooking the wide arc of Castletown Bay.

I opened a wooden gate set in the wall between two stone pillars and preceded William along a flagged path to yet another gate in an inner wall flanked by two Corinthian columns surmounted by a pair of granite globes. Beyond this second gate was a fine stretch of velvety lawn bordered by flower beds. The flagged path continued in a straight line to the front door. It was indeed a property of some consequence.

I gave a couple of resounding knocks on the brass lion-head knocker and, in a very short time, the door swung open and a stooped elderly manservant appeared. He smiled primly as we gave our names.

"You are expected" he said with a decorous bow, and led the way across an oak panelled hall to a door on our right. He gave a light knock, opened the door and stood respectfully aside for us to enter.

Mr and Mrs Christian were sitting one on either side of a crackling fire in a pleasant but rather dark room with two long windows whose light was obscured by the dark branches of trees outside. Nevertheless, it was a comfortable room, well furnished and smelling sweetly from a silver bowl full of lily of the valley set on a low table near the fire. Mr Christian, a big man of commanding presence, hook-nosed, with tufted eyebrows over shrewd grey eyes, got up, hurried towards us and shook hands.

"So you have arrived in good time for dinner" he said. "Can you wait that long, or would you like something to eat now? Ah, you have lunched at Peel. Well, you will enjoy your dinner the more for waiting". Then, turning to his wife, "Mary, this is Myles", he said, "whom I have met several times at his grandfather's house and this must be his cousin, William. We both nodded and smiled in agreement, and trusted he was well.

Mrs Christian, a small, pretty but rather dumpy woman, put down some embroidery she was working on, and rose to greet us. "You will be thirsty after your long ride", she said, and asked the manservant to bring up a tankard of ale

21

apiece. We sat to drink it on a cushioned seat that ran under the windows, and chatted together about this and that. Mr Christian asked how my grandfather did, and said how sorry he was that there was no stabling available at Knockrushen. This was because the stable was being re-roofed and would not be in use for at least another month.

Mrs Christian hoped we would enjoy our studies at the grammar school and asked if we knew any of the pupils there. I told her we did not. Then the manservant appeared again to take us to our bedroom. It was situated at the very top of the house, a long narrow room, sparsely furnished with two truckle beds, a couple of stools, a clothes press and washing stand. A window set high in the gable end of the house looked out over an apple orchard and, beyond the Stack rock and Poylvaish, to the little fishing village of Port St Mary. Further to seaward, lay the Calf of Man and the Chicken Rock, with its little hole in the middle, all surrounded by an unbelievably blue sea. I had pulled a stool to the window and was standing on it to see as far as I could. I stayed a long time gazing out on this fine panorama, until William reminded me we must wash and change for dinner. Our luggage had been sent for, unpacked and put away, and our nightshirts were laid out on the beds.

The washing stand held a jug and basin, soap and towels, and after we had washed and tidied ourselves, we returned downstairs.

At the dining table, William made himself most agreeable, regaling our host and hostess with charming little anecdotes about his mother and sisters.

Then, after dinner, back in the drawing room, he flattered them, fetching cushions to place at their backs, ever solicitous for their comfort. Amiable and eager to please as he was, they were both captivated by him. They did not, however, take to me quite so well for, feeling a little homesick, and ill at ease in my new surroundings, I hardly opened my mouth at all.

We spent an hour or so playing card games before the fire. Then Mr Christian, who had been a soldier, and in his youth had fought many battles on the continent of Europe alongside the Dutch army against Spain, entertained us with stories of his military exploits. He was a splendid raconteur and I was fascinated by his knowledge of the art of war. He spoke with authority about the disposition of troops, of mighty armed forces, their great triumphs and small defeats, and the subterfuge and ploys used to gull the enemy. I was spellbound, and could have listened with interest all night, but Mrs Christian thought we looked tired and, handing us each a lighted candle, packed us off to bed before ten o'clock.

As soon as the bedroom door closed behind us, William discarded his party manners, ignoring me as completely as if I were not there at all. He undressed quickly, blew out his candle and jumped into bed. Quite soon he was snoring away fit to beat the band. I lay awake for some time, listening to the plaintive cry of a curlew winging its way across the bay, and the gentle lap-lap-lap of waves moving against nearby rocks.

It was all very pleasant and peaceful here, yet I had a vague feeling of unease. It was awkward to have to share a room with someone as irritating as William.

22

CHAPTER FIVE

The next morning, as soon as we had finished breakfast, William and I set off along the Scarlett Road on our way to school.

It was a glorious morning, bright and breezy, the tang of seaweed strong on the air. A few brown-sailed fishing boats were already out in the bay, rising and dipping gracefully as they cut their way through cresting blue water, and everywhere flocks of gulls were sweeping and turning against a cloudless sky.

We did not speak much, for we were both a little apprehensive as to how we would fare as new students. The standard of education required at the grammar school was, we had heard, extremely high.

We skirted the market place, empty now of yesterday's gay crowd, and passed by Castle Rushen, its grey stone walls tinted pale yellow in the early morning sun, then turned right, through a narrow entry into School Lane, presently coming to a halt before the town church of St Mary which also housed the grammar school. It was a sturdy building of weathered limestone, standing a little back from the road, and within sight and sound of the sea.

Rather diffidently, I tugged at a rope which hung in a domed porch over the door, and a bell clanged loudly from a little belfry in the roof. By now ten or a dozen boys were lined up behind us, and quite soon the headmaster appeared in the doorway and waved us inside.

Mr Clucas was a small man, rotund and stocky, with a high domed forehead and hooded, watchful eyes in a plum-shaped face. He drew William and me to one side as the other boys filed past him imo a long, raftered, schoolroom with only two small windows set high at each end to allow daylight to filter through. It was full of the smell of burning wax from the many candles resting on shelves around the room, and also on the lofty window ledges. One wall was taken up by three open arches of red and yellow sandstone which gave on to various ecclesiastical offices. Mr Clucas, with quick buoyant steps, took us through one of these into his study and disposed us on a stool apiece. Then, sitting at a desk littered with books, he leaned back, finger tips together, and studied us.

Turning first to me, he asked what reading I had done, and if I knew any language other than English. Before I had a chance to reply, William broke in eagerly. He was a great reader, he said, and reeled off the titles of a number of books I had never even heard of, adding that he also had a good knowledge of both French and Latin.

Mr Clucas gazed at him affably. "That is what I like to hear", he said, and straight away put a question to him in French. For an instant William was at a loss, then his reply came hesitantly and, to my mind, not quite correctly.

There was a silence. The headmaster was frowning. He seemed puzzled and a little disappointed in him. "It will do," he said, "but your accent is not of the best". Next he asked him to conjugate a Latin verb, listening intently for his reply with raised eyebrows and his head cocked a little to one side.

William looked confused and, after a word or two, fell silent, with his eyes staring at the ceiling as if for inspiration. He was opening and shutting his mouth like a stranded fish, unable to continue.

"Not very good" said Mr Clucas with a deep sigh. "I am afraid I shall have to start at the very beginning with your Latin." William blushed and gave him a sheepish embarrassed smile, his assurance completely gone.

Then it was my turn and when, at the end of the brief examination, Mr Clucas stretched out a hand and patted my arm and said "You have been well taught, my boy," I felt a surge of gratitude for the good grounding I had been given by my former teacher, the vicar of Jurby.

Without more ado, Mr Clucas came from behind his desk and took us, first into a small cloakroom where we put on the black wide-sleeved gowns and square caps which were obligatory wear at the school, then back into the main schoolroom.

The other scholars were sitting on long benches drawn lengthwise down the room — before each boy was a wooden desk furnished with quill, pens, ink and sanding jars. As we entered, the boys stood for a moment and murmured a greeting which Mr Clucas acknowledged briefly, then installed us in two vacant seats at the end of one of the benches. Without wasting any time, he began to allocate tasks to each scholar in turn.

From the beginning I found him an able teacher, who would not tolerate laziness or insubordination. His main aim in life was to enlighten and inform every boy in his care. He did this in a quiet compelling way and, during my stay at his school, he taught me to think, sharpened my wits and gave me new ideas. Throughout all my life, I have had reason to feel greatly indebted to him.

My first few weeks there, however, were far from happy. My efforts to make friends with the other boys between classes, when we walked together in the playground or when we took lunch at Mr Clucas's house on The Parade, were thwarted by William's ill-natured remarks. Up to his old tricks, he constantly poked fun at my red hair and lack of height and did it in a clever amusing way, which made them all laugh but made me feel inept and stupid.

It was all very hard to bear and my only comfort in these dark days I found in my little mare, Peggy. Each afternoon, without fail, William and I went to attend to our horses and, as soon as I entered the stables, Peggy would turn her head and whinny softly in welcome, almost as if she knew I was in need of friendship. Indeed at that time I felt she was the only friend I had. William usually took his horse "Drifter" out along the Arbory Road to Strandhall and across the beach at Gansey, but Peggy and I made off for Langness every time. We would set off from the stables together, Peggy pacing forward with neck arched proudly as if she had royalty on her back. Then, as we came in sight of the little fishing village of Derbyhaven, she invariably broke into a canter, and went like the wind until we reached the point of Langness. Here I would rein her in, to sit gazing over the wide expanse of sea. The smell of it on the air, the salt tang of it on my lips and the spectacle of tall ships, with great wind-filled sails, gliding slowly away on the horizon never failed to lift my spirits.

It was a great relief to be away from William. He was, I thought, the most unpleasnt fellow I had ever come across. I would very much have liked to punch his nose, but I had sense enough to know I could not tackle anyone as big as he was. Instead I pretended not to be put out, however much he made fun of me. Nevertheless, I was finding it a strain and the short afternoon break away from his company cheered me immensely. After a time I would wheel round and return to Knockrushen in time for dinner, if not completely happy, at least in a more tranquil frame of mind.

CHAPTER SIX

Alas, I was not tranquil for long and any peace of mind ended abruptly one afternoon, just as school was over for the day. We were all surging through the door into the road outside, when William came bustling towards me accompanied by his special friend, a tall thick-set, black-browed youth named Maddrell. He was smiling blandly.

"We were wondering, Myles," he said, his voice loud and penetrating so that all could hear, "if you would join us in a little experiment? Since you are so small, we feel it would be easy to lift you a few feet into the air on the palms of our hands. To do this, you would have to place one foot on my right hand and the other foot on Maddrell's left hand." "You will be quite safe I assure you," Maddrell put in loftily.

By now the other boys had gathered round to watch the proceedings, but I felt vaguely uneasy and hesitated for a moment or two. Then, noticing William's sneering expression at my reluctance to do as he asked, I stooped down and took off my boots. I would not have him think me a coward. William and Maddrell bent down low and held out their hands. I placed my feet on them and folded my arms to keep a good balance. As I did so, William was smiling to himself, and I did not like his smile. Then the spectators let out a wild cheer as I was raised aloft, high above their shoulders. Suddenly, and at precisely the same moment, both boys withdrew their hands and I fell flat on my face on the gravelly road.

For a second or two I lay still, hurt and dazed with pain. My nose was bleeding and blood was pouring from my mouth, but my tormentors thought it a great joke, and went off with the rest of the boys roaring with laughter.

Sick with rage, I got up and, holding a handkerchief to my face, stumbled slowly along School Lane, my heart bitter and cold with loneliness. Turning the corner into Chapel Lane, I saw a tall young fellow coming towards me, hands in pockets and whistling tunelessly to himself. When he spotted me, he stopped in his tracks and looked me over with a mixture of surprise and gentle sympathy.

"Been in a fight?" he asked. "Not exactly" I replied. He had spoken in Manx Gaelic, and it was second nature to me to reply in the same tongue, for I had been familiar with it from my earliest years. Kitty and George Quayle, and indeed all the workers at Ellanbane, spoke little else, using English as a foreign language. My father and grandfather, however, had always insisted that I spoke English when in their company, yet I loved the slow musical inflections of Manx. For me it was the language of home.

"Well then," the young fellow went on, "tell me what happened to get you in this state?"

With a half sob and feeling near to tears, I blurted out the whole sorry story. As I was speaking, he leaned forward and gazed at me with a look of dawning recognition.

"I remember you now" he exclaimed. "This cousin of yours was the fellow that thumped the young lad last market day as you were crossing the square".

I nodded and stared back at him. "And you were one of the gang that barred our way."

"Yes, and your cousin was lucky not to have been given a good hiding."

"He well deserved one" I answered.

There was a slight pause, then he gave me a comradely grin. "I think it would be a good idea", he said, "for you to come home with me, then you could clean yourself up a bit."

I was glad to agree, for I felt battered and dirty. "You are very kind" I said gratefully, as he turned back and took me to his house in Parliament Lane. He was a cheery soul and chattered all the way there. He asked my name, and told me he was Joe Karran. He explained that his mother was dead and that he lived with his father, an inshore fisherman. They owned a small boat and earned a fair living fishing for cod and mackerel. They also had some lobster pots set in the bay, and his father was out there now putting fresh bait in them.

His house, when we came to it, was a small whitewashed cottage. The door opened directly into a small living room with an earth floor and smelled strongly of fish. We continued through an open door at the back of the living room into a dark, dingy scullery. On a rickety table was a bowl of water, some soap and a flannel. My nose and mouth had stopped bleeding, and I stripped down to my waist and bathed my sore face carefully. It was caked with dried blood and the cold water was very soothing. Joe handed me a towel and I soon made myself presentable again. Meanwhile, Joe had been observing me closely.

"You have a strong little body" he said. "You should learn to wrestle. Big fellows used to bully me too when I was a small boy, but they soon stopped when I learned to handle myself properly. My father taught me to wrestle. He learned all the tricks of the trade when he worked on a Cumberland farm in his young days. So what do you say to taking a few lessons from him? In no time at all you would be able to master fellows twice your size, even that big cousin of yours, for instance.

Joe sounded so confident that my heart leapt with joy. At that moment, my dearest wish was to beat William into submission, to make him cry out for mercy.

"I would like that, Joe," I said, "more than anything else on earth."

"Right" said Joe: "come back here to-night around about 8 o'clock and we will begin to lick you into shape."

So punctually at eight I presented myself again at Joe's cottage.

27

CHAPTER SEVEN

He greeted me warmly and introduced me to his father, Edward Karran, a stocky deep-chested man, with grizzled fair hair and sun-wrinkled blue eyes, set far apart in a bronzed face. As we shook hands, he was looking me over shrewdly.

"So you would like to learn to wrestle" he observed, pursing his lips and laying a hand on my shoulder.

"Yes" I said, and told him I had a cousin, a big fellow, who seemed to bear me a permanent grudge. "He is a bully", I went on, "and I would like to be able to defend myself in the event of a tussle with him. Will you teach me?"

A slow smile spread over his face. "Aye that I will, and put my money on you too."

Joe, who was standing between us, grinned broadly, and gave me a sly wink. "I knew he would" he said, and went over to pull a rag-rug from before the fire into the centre of the room. On it they both set to work to teach me the strategic mysteries of wrestling.

First of all I had to do exercises to strengthen my neck muscles. "A strong neck", said Edward, "is most essential."

Then I had to learn the correct wrestling stance, feet well apart and in line, knees bent and loose, and how to hold my hands in the "Butchers grip", one of the initial holds.

At the end of the evening I was wet with sweat. The desire to succeed in this branch of the art of self-defence was like a fire within me, and I was determined to work at it with all my might. So every evening throughout the whole of June and July, with the exception of Sundays, I went to the little house in Parliament Lane for a few bouts with the Karrans. Consequently I soon became proficient in the simpler throws. The "cross buttock", "double-thigh pick-up" and the "flying mare" gave me no trouble, but it was a long time before I mastered the lethal "quarter and half-nelson" and the "cradle hold".

Meanwhile I could feel myself growing stronger and fitter almost daily, and I grew an inch taller as well. As an added bonus, a warm friendship sprang up between me and the Karrans. They were both simple, likeable fellows, and I always felt at home and sure of a welcome at their house. During the summer months school finished at three o'clock so, when time and tide permitted, they took me fishing with them.

I think if I live to be a hundred I will never forget those golden happy days.

Stepping down the green oozy harbour steps onto the boat, the air full of the mewing of gulls as we got under way, then, gliding alongside the lofty sea wall into the rolling sun-spangled waters of Castletown Bay, letting down lobster pots on to the sea bed as we went and drawing up others with lobsters imprisoned inside them.

Usually we dropped anchor just under the lea of Langness point and, baiting our hooks with fat lugworm, we would fish for hour after glorious hour. Then, on warm summer evenings full of a bright sunset glow, finally return to harbour with a good catch, tired but satisfied.

Even now, years and years after, I remember with longing the beauty of that coastline as Edward swung the boat round to make port. On one side the jagged Stack Rock standing out of the sea, blackish brown with seaweed and lashed with foam around its edges, and on the other the great castle, towering over the huddled roofs of the little grey town like a hen amongst her chickens. Away in the distance softly curving purple hills, with long shadows on them forming a gentle background, and over all the fretful wailing cries of the gulls and the sound and smell of the sea.

During all this time, indeed ever since he had played his shabby trick on me, I had steered clear of William. I did not pointedly ignore him, but spoke to him only when it was strictly necessary to do so. He was, as I have mentioned before, a great favourite with Mr and Mrs Christian with whom he always made himself particularly agreeable, and I had a suspicion that they noted and disapproved of my unfriendly attitude towards him. Therefore, I could not help feeling pleased when one evening, as we sat together in the drawing room, through no effort of mine, they were made aware of the reason for my coolness.

Mrs Christian was engaged on some needlework, and I was listening intently as Mr Christian held forth on the tactics and strategy of warfare, a subject close to his heart and one that never failed to interest me. William was sitting at a side-table smiling to himself over a drawing he was making. He was an excellent artist and Mr Clucas had fastened many of his drawings to the walls at school, where they were much admired.

During a lull in Mr Christian's discourse, William passed his work to me with a supercilious smile. "Look at that" he said. What he was showing me was a clever and cruel caricature of myself and I blushed with chagrin.

He had pictured me standing erect, nose in the air and arms folded, on two great disembodied palms. I was gazing upwards with a sanctimonious expression, my head ringed around with a wobbly halo.

"Look at the other side now" murmured William. I did so, and there I was again, but this time flat on my face, the two hands suspended above me, and clapped together as if in applause. Underneath he had written "How are the mighty fallen".

I was gazing down at it, my face flushed with anger, when Mrs Christian, seeing I was upset, leaned forward and stretched out her hand.

"May I see it, Myles," she said. Without a word, I passed it to her. She scrutinised it carefully, turning it over a time or two, then started to question William.

"What is it all about?" she asked.

He gave a quick contemptuous smile.

"It is just a momento of an experiment in which Myles was involved."

"Tell me about it" she persisted.

He was silent for a few seconds then explained exactly, and in detail, all that had happened. He giggled now and then as he recalled my horrified expression as I fell to the ground.

Mrs Christian, looking at him with angry eyes, passed the drawing to her husband, who glanced at it briefly, tore it across, then threw it onto the fire.

"That was a cruel thing to do" said Mrs Christian. "I think you owe an apology to Myles."

William, looking fixedly at her, yawned, shrugged his shoulders and said nothing.

All of a sudden there was a feeling of tension in the room. Mr Christian hurled himself up and went and stood before William, glaring belligerently at him. "Now then my boy. Apologise to Myles this instant or else leave my house in the morning."

William, looking a little scared, hung his head and mumbled an apology. Mr Christian, slightly mollified, returned to his chair but he was still annoyed and red in the face. "I am afraid I must revise my former good opinion of you, William," he said. "That was an intolerable trick to play on Myles and I trust nothing of the like will happen again between you."

Just then supper was announced, and the whole affair was for the moment forgotten but, when no-one was looking, William flashed me a look of such concentrated hatred that I knew with certainty it would not be long before he planned some other scheme by which to humiliate me.

CHAPTER EIGHT

Soon afterwards came the end of term examinations and, when they were over, Mr Clucas sent us off on a country ramble while he assessed the results. He chose a pleasant route for us, which was to follow the course of the Silverburn, from Castletown via Ballasalla to Rushen Abbey, then back by the main road through Cross Four Ways and past Malew Parish Church.

So, starting at the upper harbour, we set off in little groups of two's and three's. First, under a low weatherbeaten bridge lined with oozing foliage and smelling oddly of mould, then along a narrow footpath beside the river. It was a small river, only a few yards wide, boulder strewn and closely confined between earth banks overgrown with willow herb and wild rhubarb. It meandered gently through rough reedy pastures, well stocked with sheep and dotted about with thistles and great clumps of ragwort. The air was gloriously fresh, and the atmosphere cordial amongst us, as we made our way in single file upstream through patches of young bracken and sweet smelling gorse. At one point I lagged behind the others to watch some fine fat trout as they lay almost motionless beneath smooth boulders in mid-stream, while the water rippled and gurgled busily around them.

Then I heard one of the boys shout "Come on you with the red hair", and I hurried off to join the rest of the party. They were waiting at a stile strategically placed at a bend in the river beside a small waterfall. As I approached, I heard William say something which seemed to be a signal for a general movement to gather round him.

When I was within two yards of the group, his henchman, Maddrell, shouted in a loud mocking voice "Here comes our little cock sparrow".

I paused for an instant. They were all staring hard at me as if I had done something terrible. I looked doubtfully from one to another. "What is the matter?" I asked. "What have I done?" No one spoke.

Then, suddenly bold, I elbowed my way through them and was just about to climb over the stile when William thrust out a leg to bar my way. Without hesitating, I grabbed his foot and twisted it slowly but firmly. With a yell of rage he tumbled to the ground, but in a second was on his feet again and advanced towards me, head lowered menacingly like a frenzied bull, but I was ready for him. I stuck out my fist and hit him a solid blow right between the eyes, then caught him in a wrestling hold as he put out his arm to grab me. Snatching his wrist, I half turned my back and threw him over my shoulder slamming him hard on the ground. He lay there winded amidst urgent calls to get up and fight, but

William was finished and he knew it.

There was a murmur of surprise and some jeering as the little crowd pressed forward to get a better view. "Come on now William" someone shouted. "Have another try. You are big enough to finish Myles with one hand tied behind you".

Eventually he rose to his feet looking crestfallen, and was about to walk away, but the boys shoved him relentlessly towards me again. He hung his head. "I have had enough" he muttered.

"But for how long?" I asked and met him with a solid body punch. He sank to his knees gulping for air, hardly any breath left in his body. I stood over him and held my fist above his head. "Now say you will stop persecuting me or I will punch your nose into the back of your head".

"I promise" he whispered hoarsely, and I helped him to his feet.

Staggering a little, he slunk away to cries of "Hurrah for Myles", and suddenly I had become something of a hero.

From that day onwards, I was held in some esteem, which made life at school a good deal more pleasant. Incidentally, I had no more trouble from William, at least not until many years later, when he was instrumental in dealing me a bitter blow. Even now, I find it hard to forgive him for that evil deed, for it has affected the well-being of my entire family ever since. However, to get back to my story – William appeared at the dinner table that evening sporting a couple of black eyes: one eye was almost completely closed. Mr Christian glanced sharply at him.

"Been fighting, William?" he asked.

"Yes" said William, red-faced with embarrassment. "With one of the boys at school, I suppose?"

"With Myles" said William, his eyes downbent, his head sunk on his chest.

At this Mr Christian threw back his head and laughed until the tears ran down his cheeks. He crashed his fist onto the table in a paroxysm of mirth. "I cannot believe it" he cried again and again. "Big William getting two black eyes from little Myles. Upon my soul, here is another David and Goliath".

Even Mrs Christian was smiling, and I found it in my heart to feel just a little sorry for William.

Next day we returned to Ellanbane for the long summer vacation. We were both a little subdued, but neither of us showed any sign of animosity as we rode together through the lush summer landscape.

The previous day's battle had somehow cleared the air between us and, although we never became really friendly, we treated one another with a kind of courteous toleration. William now knew that I could look after myself in a fight, and this fact gave me considerable satisfaction.

It was a glorious day, and I felt my heart swell with joy as we travelled homewards past fields golden with harvest and little whitewashed crofters' cottages, their whiteness dazzling in the sunshine. Crimson fuchsias flamed in the hedges, and the fragrant summer air was alive with country sounds and smells. Honeysuckle and cut hay, the gentle cropping sound of cattle, the humming of bees, the singular whirring sound of pheasants, rising up now and then from deep tree-lined hedges, and over all the indefinable green smell of sun-warmed grass.

As before, we broke our journey at Peel to feed and water the horses and eat a good meal ourselves, then continued on our way through the little hamlets of Kirk Michael, Ballaugh and Sulby and on to the Lezayre road with the Nappin ridge to our right, heather covered now and purple against a pale blue sky.

Turning into the leafy drive leading to Ellanbane, I had the curious feeling of never having been away. The past few months receded into a kind of limbo almost as if they had been experienced by another person.

Although it was barely dusk when we arrived, the curtains were drawn all over the house. The front door stood open and the hall was bathed in a golden light from candles standing in wall sconces and on several small tables. My grandfather, Aunt Bella, Rose and Barbara welcomed us warmly, and I truly believe they were glad to see us back. I found everything greatly changed. All was very grand – silver sparkled, furniture shone, carpets had been cleaned and refurbished, but somehow the homeliness had completely vanished. I missed the old happy-go-lucky atmosphere. Sadly, I knew with certainty I would never again sit easy and comfortable in the chimney corner.

That first evening my grandfather said he wanted to see me before I went to bed so, after supper, I went along to the little room he used as a study. I knocked and entered. He was sitting in his high backed chair leaning back, hands folded loosely across his chest, his eyes as usual appraising and alert. He indicated a stool beside him and, as I sat down, he laid an arm across my shoulders.

For an instant I saw my father in his patrician features, in his kind expression and gentle smile. Yet never before had I noticed this resemblance. Was he so like my father? I asked myself, my father whom I had loved so dearly, or was it because I had often sat like this to my lessons with him in this very room?

My grandfather cleared his throat and began: "I want to have a talk with you, Myles, and it will take some little time. I have asked you here tonight", he said, "in order to lay before you the ambitions I hold for your future as heir to my estates both here and in Lancashire".

"I will be glad to listen to your views, sir", I said, "and will try to fulfil your wishes."

His gratification at my remark was obvious, as a smile flickered across his face. "First of all I must tell you something of our family history. You have, up to now, been kept a little ignorant on that subject, mainly on account of your youth, but now it is high time you were enlightened on several matters which are very important to me." He was stroking his beard and staring thoughtfully into the distance. "The Standishes spring from an illustrious stock entitled to bear Arms" he said. "Our crest is, as you know, 'a hare with a rat in its mouth proper'". I nodded: I knew it well for it was engraved on much of our silver and carved over the archway above the oak staircase.

"We have been settled", he went on, "for generations at Ormskirk in Lancashire, in the hundred of West Derby, holding rich farmland in Burscough, Croston, Mandesley, Wrighton and Newburgh and also owning several coal

33

mines in the same area. So, after my death, you will become a very rich man. It is my wish, therefore, that you begin to learn how to look after your inheritance, to understand farm management and to guard the Standish lands with your life. I trust that one day you will make a good marriage and father sons capable of bearing the Standish name with honour."

Here he paused for a moment or two, his expression now grown serious, and a little anxious. He was looking away from me and frowning slightly. "There is, however," he said at last, "another important matter about which you must be made aware. It will probably come as a great surprise to you to learn that I am a totally committed Roman Catholic, albeit a secret one, as was your father before you. These are dangerous times for those of my Faith, Myles, so I must always appear to be a staunch Protestant, attending Church regularly in order to prevent our lands from being sequestered and also to avoid molestation. Notwithstanding, I am still able to hear Mass several times in the year, as a priest from the English mission comes as often as possible to perform the rite, and this gives me great spiritual comfort and immense happiness."

This was indeed astounding news, and I could hardly believe my ears. I gazed up at him with a puzzled frown. "But never in my whole life have I seen a priest at Ellanbane" I cried.

My grandfather gave me a knowing smile. "Indeed you have", he said, "and also dined with him many times. He is our good friend, Mr McAuley, who comes in the guise of family lawyer, and stays with us for several days as an honoured guest."

I stared at him dumbfounded. I knew and liked Mr McAuley very well indeed, but it was difficult for me to think of him as being what Protestants call a Papist priest. He had no special aura of sanctity about him but was always jolly and full of fun – a most friendly man. "But most of our relations are Protestants are they not?" I asked.

"Just so" said my grandfather. "Several of them are even Church of England clergymen, but I have always loved the old religion, and adhered to it. It is the Faith of our fathers: to my mind the only true religion, and it is my dearest wish that one day you too will embrace it and become a Roman."

I shook my head emphatically. "When my father died, I ceased to believe in God" I said. He patted my arm affectionately. "You are young now and filled with the intolerance of youth, but I feel sure that, as you grow older, your ideas will alter. One more thing, however, I must ask of you. It is that you will have a private talk with Mr McAuley when he visits us in a couple of weeks' time. He will be able to instruct you much better than I on the tenets of our Faith, and I will be obliged if you will give the matter serious consideration. Many Standish men have fought valiantly for the Faith, even died for it. We have been a fairly hot headed lot, and have always bred brave soldiers. One of them, Robert de Standish, helped to slay Wat Tyler at Smithfield away back in 1381 and was knighted for his services. In fact, the history of the Standishes is a history of valour and hot blood. We are also allied to a branch of the great Stanley family,

34

Kings of Mann, through the marriage of my uncle, Thomas Standish, to Joanna Stanley. It was he that persuaded me to buy Ellanbane after the dissolution of the monasteries, both here and at Rushen Abbey, and to take over the stewardship of all the Stanley property in this island. This I was glad to do, for there is less harassment of the Catholic Church here and, if by any chance my allegiance to Rome was discovered, the punishment would be less severe than in England." He sighed deeply, and there was a long silence.

Then, smiling at me, he said "Well, that is all I have to say to you, my boy, save to remind you to keep my secret most carefully, which I am quite sure you will, but I beg of you to be ever vigilant. These are difficult times for me." He stood up and bade me goodnight and, as we shook hands, said "You are an excellent listener, Myles, and I hope our talk will bear much fruit."

Going up to my room my mind was in a turmoil for, while my grandfather had been holding forth about my future, I was suddenly made aware of what I really wanted to do with my life. Alas, for I loved him dearly and would have liked to have fallen in with his wishes, I realised it was not the business of running a large estate that appealed to me. Instead, I was fired by an ambition to become a soldier like so many of my forebears. I was thinking how wonderful it would be to sail away from this small island, to do battle in faraway lands and, maybe, to discover some new exciting country.

I think perhaps Mr Christian's tales of his wartime exploits had sown the first seeds of this longing for adventure. But now I also had the example of brave Standish soldiers to emulate and, deep in my heart, was the sure and certain knowledge that one day I would make this dream come true. That night I slept like a log. It was good to be back in my own room again without the restricting presence of William – it was like entering port after a storm.

At first light I got up to jog around the estate on Peggy to see again all the old familiar landmarks, the ancient trees, little leafy lanes and byways hedged with bramble and hawthorn, arriving back in time for breakfast. This was a noisy meal with Rose and Barbara teasing William and me unmercifully. They were making arrangments for a picnic on Scacafell, but I excused myself and said I would be spending the day with George and Kitty Quayle.

"Which was just as I thought" said Aunt Bella, giving me an amiable pat on the back. "Away you go" she added.

So, as soon as the meal was finished, I set off with a lift of the heart along the road to Glentrammon.

As I neared the low rambling farmhouse, I could see Scamp lying full length in a patch of sunlight before the open front door. I gave a short, sharp whistle and, within seconds, he was bounding towards me. Soon he was jumping up, licking my hands and face, making little yapping noises and nuzzling his head against my legs. Then he rolled onto his back and looked up at me with adoring eyes. As I stooped to rub his chest, suddenly I was full of emotion and found myself near to tears. Then Kitty appeared, wiping sudsy hands on her apron. She came quickly and put her arms around me, kissing me tenderly, and I was a little boy again.

CHAPTER NINE

It happened to be Kitty's butter-making day and, to help her, I took a stint at the churn which had been pulled out, from its usual place in a recess by the fireplace, into the middle of the kitchen. I sat before it on a low stool with Scamp lying curled up beside me, and set to work plunging the dasher up and down while Kitty, brisk and methodical as ever, washed dishes and set things to rights. She was talking all the time, regaling me with snippets of local gossip. Twins had been born to a neighbouring farmer's wife, one old man had died and three weddings had taken place in my absence. The philandering Jacques had suddenly disappeared from the district, and Voirrey Mylecraine was now being courted by a prosperous sheep farmer from Andreas.

"A well set up fellow he is" said Kitty. "Her father likes him, and has given his blessing, and they are getting married in the spring."

As an afterthought she let fall that George was hard at work this morning in the harvest field, and I guessed she was hoping that I would give him a helping hand later on.

"There is nothing I should enjoy more", I said quite truthfully too, "than to do some harvesting." She gave me a grateful smile, and began packing all kinds of eatables into a large basket.

I found it very pleasant sitting there in the big farm kitchen, listening to Kitty and working away at the churn. The heavily-hinged door stood open and a pool of sunshine lay on the stone-flagged floor, and shone on the whitewashed walls. A delicious aromatic scent from lavender and gilly flowers wafted in from the tiny garden, and the air was alive with birdsong and the drone of bees. A wave of happiness went through me, and I was thinking I would be content to stay forever in this restful homely spot. The butter came at last. Kitty worked it in a bowl, packed it into a crock, poured buttermilk into several earthenware jugs and scalded out the churn, then handed me the basket covered with a white cloth. "You will find George in the top meadow", she said, "and I will join you as soon as I have fed the calves".

So I set off along the earthy-smelling well trodden path, with Scamp trotting along beside me, and went through a gap in the hedge into the "Top meadow". George did not see me at first, and I stood for a moment or two admiring the strength of his broad shoulders as he wielded a sickle with a precise and rhythmic movement of his whole body.

He must have sensed my presence, for suddenly he turned and, spotting me, laid down the sickle and, with a great shout of welcome, came over to greet me, a broad smile crinkling his good humoured face.

"About time you came back from foreign parts" he said, his voice loud and exuberant, as he gave me several friendly slaps on the back.

We went to sit under the blackthorn hedge to talk and wait for Kitty. Soon she appeared, and we ate a splendid meal from the basket. Soda cakes spread with soft yellow butter, hunks of crumbly cheese, hard boiled eggs and slices of apple pie. All washed down with home-brewed ale from a leather bottle. Everything tasted delicious. I think the glory of the day gave it a special piquancy. A lark was singing out of sight in a lightly fleeced blue sky, the sun shone warm on our faces and the air was soft and balmy. At the bottom of the basket Kitty had tucked away a parcel of meat scraps for Scamp, and, after he had wolfed them down, he ambled off to nose after rats in the hedge bottom, and slake his thirst in a little river that ran along one side of the field.

After we had finished eating, George went back to his sickle: I gathered the cut corn into sheaves and Kitty bound them with corn stalks. We worked for hours like this until all was finished, with sheaves stooked in serried ranks right across the field, pale gold now where it had been shorn of its crop. It was after eight o'clock when we left for home, but the sun was still above the horizon and the air remained warm and fragrant in the heat of the evening.

"We will start work in the home fields tomorrow" said George as we parted, taking it for granted I would be there to help. And so, for almost the whole of the holidays, I went each day to lend a hand with the harvest or anything else that needed doing. Usually I went to bed early, pleasantly tired after a long day's toil, and it was only at breakfast and dinner that I saw William and the girls. They teased me a lot and nicknamed me "Farmer Myles", but it was good natured teasing and we were all easy and friendly together when we met.

Then one evening, unannounced and without fuss, Mr McAuley appeared at the dinner table. He was, as always, kind and friendly – a big man, broad of shoulder and slim of hip, with alert gray eyes and a humourous mouth. During the meal, he was asking my grandfather pertinent questions about farming methods on the Island and the state of the economy, subjects in which my grandfather was much involved.

I kept stealing a furtive glance at him now and then, for I still found it hard to believe he was a seminary priest. Once he met my gaze and gave me a confidential wink, and I was immediately aware that he knew I was in the secret.

As we left the table, my grandfather caught my arm and asked me not to go quite so early to the farm next morning. "Mr McAuley would like to have a talk with you on matters connected with the estate, and for this reason I want you to come to my room not later than eleven o'clock" he said.

So, a little before the appointed hour, I went up to my grandfather's bedroom. I turned the knob, but the door was locked, and I was just about to knock for admittance when I heard a low murmuring voice from within, running on and on monotonously. Then it stopped. There was a muffled movement and a tinkling sound. I pricked up my ears as the muttering began again. The intoned words were in Latin, and it dawned on me then that I was listening to a celebration of the Catholic Mass.

Suddenly the voice ceased and, after a moment or two of absolute silence, my grandfather opened the door. His face was suffused with happiness. Never before had I seen him so elated. He touched his lips with a finger to remind me to be discreet as he held the door open for me to enter. It was quite dark inside. The curtains were closely drawn and the room was heavy with the smell of incense. Two candles, giving a flickering light, stood on a low table drawn against the far wall on which a large brass crucifix had been fastened. On a smaller table was a statue of "Our Lady".

Mr McAuley was standing before the improvised altar, busily packing some small objects into a travelling bag. As I entered he turned and, with an observant smile, watched me walk towards him. Without speaking, he laid a hand on my shoulder and drew me towards the window seat. Sitting beside me there, he drew out a silver crucifix from beneath his soutane and, holding it between thumb and forefinger, he spoke of the Faith that was in him, explaining everything carefully, slowly and very intensely.

He began by telling me that he had been educated at Douai and had trained there as a missionary priest, one who was sent regularly across the Channel for the preservation and augmentation of the Faith of Catholics in England. "But it is a dangerous life" he said, and here his expression grew grave, his voice controlled and a little fearful. "For, if I am discovered celebrating Mass, it is certain I will be hanged, drawn and quartered, without the benefit of being put to death first." I shuddered at the thought, and marvelled at a Faith that could defy the laws of the land in the face of such terrible punishment.

Then he went on to speak of the love of God, the sacrifice of the Sacrament, the forgiveness of sins, of Heaven, Hell and Purgatory. He was so earnest, his arguments so reasoned and lucid, that I could have said like King Agrippa "Almost thou persuadest me". But there was a certain hard core of disbelief in my heart that I was unable to overcome. I could not be dishonest and pretend to a belief I did not have, even though I should have liked to have pleased him. I told him this, and he shook his head: "No, Myles, that would not do at all," he said gently, "but I shall pray for you. Great things have been wrought by prayer." I said Goodbye to him outside the bedroom door. "God be with you, my son," he said as he pressed my hand.

"And also with you, Father" said I.

That afternoon saw the end of the Glentrammon harvest, with the corn gathered safely into the barn, and Kitty, George and I were just sitting down to an excellent celebration tea when Betsey Mylecraine walked into the warm, cheerful room. Her face was full of suppressed excitement. Kitty asked her to join us at table so, drawing up a stool, she settled herself on it and plunged straight into a piece of news which filled me with dismay.

"A Massing priest has been seen in the district" she burst out. "He was recognised in a Ramsey street by a turncoat Catholic who says he knew him in England as a missionary. He has reported him to the Captain of the Parish, but no-one seems to know where he is." Here she slewed round on her stool and gazed at me with narrowed eyes. "They say he was last seen making his way towards Ellanbane." There was a query in her voice, and I tried to throw her off scent.

"Oh that would be our family lawyer who visits us regularly to report on the Standish holdings in England". I spoke dismissively as though her obvious suspicion was stupid.

Kitty's glance met mine. "Do you mean Mr McAuley?" she asked.

I nodded.

"I knew him well when I worked at Ellanbane," she said, turning to Betsey, "and I am quite sure he is no Massing priest."

"Are you indeed" said Betsey, her voice full of disbelief, as she sat gazing at me with an inflexible stare. Then she asked if I knew of any Romish practices taking place at Ellanbane while this man was there.

I just shook my head in denial. I was afraid to speak in case alarm in my voice would give me away, for she was no fool.

Luckily George, who had been sitting very quietly up to now, suddenly broke in. "Be quiet, Aunt" he said in a harsh voice. "Myles has already told you who the man is, and both Kitty and he have said that he comes here regularly on Standish business. In any case, I have never considered you to be a particularly devout Protestant, so why are you so set against Catholics?" Scamp, who was lying under the table, on hearing the angry tone in George's voice, suddenly growled.

I looked at Betsey, sitting very upright, while George spoke to her. She was flushed with indignation, her head was thrown back, her mouth folded in a malicious smile and I felt she was capable of much evil. "We want no popery here" she cried. "We must root out these seminaries from their hiding places wherever they are, and I for one will help in any way I can to get rid of them."

George shrugged his shoulders and gave a despairing sigh. "I hate such bigotry" he said crossly. He was not a contentious man but his eyes were hostile as he stared into Betsey's outraged face.

There was a silence. Then she rose from the table and moved to the door. "I will not sit here to be insulted and browbeaten" she said and stumped off, muttering to herself as she went, then banged the door behind her.

As soon as she had gone, I told Kitty and George of Mr McAuley's true identity for I was worried. I had no one else to turn to, and I knew full well his secret would be safe with them. I enlarged on the awful fate awaiting him were he to be discovered, hoping they would offer him refuge.

"The poor man" said Kitty when I had finished speaking. She looked across at George, and there was an unspoken question in her eyes.

He nodded at her gravely, then turned to me. "Fetch the gentleman here" he said. "We can hide him in one of the outhouses until it is safe for him to return to England."

I stayed only long enough to thank them both for this generous gesture, then went hotfoot to warn my grandfather and Mr McAuley of the danger they were in, and to bring Mr McAuley to Glentrammon without delay. He agreed at once to come with me, and within an hour I was on my way back with him to Glentrammon. The moon had risen, and was shining brightly as we travelled together along the rutted lane. There was no-one about, and everywhere was peaceful and still. I was feeling quite confident that all would be well but, as we turned a bend in the lane, I was horrified to see two men standing on either side of the gate which led into the farmyard. They were a good two hundred yards away, but I could see one of them was holding aloft a great wooden mustering cross which, in case of emergency, is used on the Island as a general summons from the Captain of the Parish.

Quickly Mr McAuley thrust me behind him. "Get over the hedge Myles", he said, "and run back home as fast as you can. You cannot be identified at this distance, and I do not want to involve you or your family in my affairs."

I did as he commanded and climbed over the hedge but, instead of making for home, I crouched down out of sight and watched fearfully through a tiny interspace as the two men approached, took hold of an arm apiece and marched him away. Sick at heart, I gazed after them until they disappeared into the shadows: then, full of anxiety, I walked slowly home.

I thought it better at this juncture not to tell my grandfather what had happened, for I knew his reaction would be to saddle a horse immediately and tear after Mr McAuley and his captors, and that to my mind would be a terrible mistake. They would be only too pleased to have two lawbreakers to deal with instead of one. So I went quietly off to bed as if nothing untoward had happened, and lay there tossing and turning the whole night through. Once I fell asleep for a while, only to be troubled by a dreadful nightmare. I dreamt I was standing by as Mr McAuley's ears were cropped by two inquisitors, who then proceeded to hang and disembowel him, and I awoke with the sound of his screams reverberating in my head. I did not get to sleep again but, as soon as dawn broke, I got up and went to Glentrammon. I had to tell George and Kitty why I had failed to turn up as arranged with Mr McAuley.

I was about half-way there when I spotted George trotting towards me on the stiff farm cart laden with bundles of last year's hay. As he drew level, he pulled at his reins and stopped. I had just launched into my tale of woe when he interrupted. "I must hurry on" he said. "I have an important job to do. Kitty will tell you all about it." Then, jerking his thumb meaningfully behind him, he set off again.

I was staring after him, baffled that he did not wait to hear the reason for my non-appearance the previous evening, when I was staggered beyond belief to see the head and shoulders of Mr McAuley emerge from beneath a pile of sacks at the back of the cart. He gave me a surprisingly sweet smile as he made the sign of the cross in a kind of benediction, then submerged again beneath the sacks. For a moment I wondered if my eyes were deceiving me. I stood rooted to the spot in sheer bewilderment before setting off to look for Kitty, whom I hoped would enlighten me. I found her in the cow house. She was sitting with her head pressed against a cow's soft flank, her dexterous fingers directing a steady flow of milk into a bucket. She turned her head and smiled up at me, a bright happy smile, her expression clear and untroubled.

"Did you meet George on your way over?" she asked.

"Yes I met him" I replied as I took a milking stool from a peg, sat down beside her and looked into her eyes. "Now tell me all that has been happening here". And I listened incredulously as she told me how Mr McAuley had escaped from his captors.

"These two fellows who collared him last night", she said, "had been sent by the Governor, Cuthbert Gerard, for protection. The Governor it seems is also a secret Catholic as are all his servants. They carried the wooden cross as a blind, so that anyone they met would think they were taking a common criminal to justice. Originally their plan was to take him to Castle Rushen where he would have to be kept in hiding at some considerable risk to the Governor himself, for no Catholic is safe these days. However, when they revealed themselves to Mr McAuley and he was able to tell them he could find shelter with us, they brought him here instead. George luckily knew of a fishing boat that was to leave Ramsey this morning for Westport in Ireland, and that is where he was going when you met him, with our friend well hidden from sight. The poor man will be certain to find friends in Westport who will help him on his way back to England."

I was so pleased to hear this good news that I flung my arms around Kitty, nearly knocking over the pailful of milk. I was feeling exhilarated, mistakenly confident that, with this small success, religious prejudice could be overcome. But sadly, and I blame it on Betsey Mylecraine and her cronies, it became increasingly difficult for Catholics to attend to their religion. The whole Island was full of gossip and speculation. My grandfather was only able to attend Mass at infrequent intervals and that late at night in the crypt of the Cathedral of St Germans on Peel Island. The rite was performed by a priest who travelled from the British Isles in the guise of a strolling fiddler.

For my part, I thought I had heard the last of Mr McAuley. Then, one day, a parcel arrived for me containing several treatises on the Roman Catholic Faith, together with a covering note to say I was continually in his prayers.

CHAPTER TEN

On looking back, the year 1602 was for me an eventful one.

William and I had finished with school and William had been sent, at Aunt Bella's insistence, to study law in England. She took it for granted that, by so doing, he could eventually become a Deemster in the Manx High Court of Justice, and I agreed with her that it was a good idea. There had been some changes here at home during the past few years. George and Kitty now had a little son, just four years old. A fine lively little fellow with dark hair and a pair of mischievous brown eyes. They had named him Huan after my father, which gave me great pleasure.

Old Mylecraine had died leaving all he possessed to Voirrey, who surprisingly had quarelled with her young sheep farmer, and then taken herself off to live with some distant cousins in Devonshire. Kitty heard she was now married to the vicar of a small but prosperous parish near Dartington. Betsey Mylecraine still flourished like the green bay tree, and never seemed to look any older, although to my mind she had always been singularly unprepossessing. She was as usual a frequent visitor at Glentrammon, but when we met we rarely had much to say to one another, for there had been an unspoken hostility between us ever since the McAuley affair.

As for myself, I was kept fully occupied, for, besides working on the estate, I was now obliged to travel to England from time to time in order to supervise the running of our various holdings in Lancashire, since unfortunately our agent there had recently died.

Each time I went, I stayed at Edgeacre near Ormskirk, the home of Richard Collyson, a rich landowner friend of my grandfather. He had a young son, Arthur, a pleasant amusing fellow with whom I became particularly friendly. Indeed it was partly due to his influence that my life changed so dramatically that year. He was newly down from Oxford but, before returning home, had spent a couple of months in London staying with one of his fellow graduates. He was full of the splendid time to be had in the capital, and talked glibly of the Fortune and Globe theatres, where he had seen several performances of plays by the famous writer, Mr William Shakespeare. He had rubbed shoulders with court dandies, visited the Zoological Gardens at the tower and the monuments at Westminster, and paid a penny for a view of London from the damaged steeple of St Pauls. But most of all I was intrigued by his stories of the valiant deeds of English soldiers in foreign lands. He talked knowledgeably about the maritime adventures of Raleigh, Drake, Frobisher and many other brave men, whose names were quite strange to me.

He had a great fund of information on world affairs, and he set me thinking that I lived in a backwater where nothing of any importance occurred. In any case, for some time now I had been feeling bored with my life. I wanted more action, more excitement. At the same time I had no desire to join the idle throng that were Arthur's friends.

Instead I was bent on seeking adventure in other faraway lands. In short I had never wholly stifled the wish to become a soldier. So I made up my mind to ask my grandfather to appoint another steward in my place, thus setting me free to leave home and see the world, which in this year of Our Lord was so full of momentous and thrilling events.

I waited until the eve of my eighteenth birthday before broaching the subject. We were sitting facing each other across the dining table. Aunt Bella and the girls had left the room and there was a full decanter of wine before us, gleaming richly under the candles' soft light. After we had drunk a glass or two, I cleared my throat and told him what was in my mind. How bored I was here on the Island. How badly I wanted to be a soldier, and that I wished to leave home and join the army as soon as possible.

He listened to all I had to say with close concentration and, when I had finished speaking, he poured out another glass of wine, drank it down and set the empty glass slowly and deliberately on the table before him. Then, leaning back in his chair, his hands clasped over his paunch, he gave me a critical stare, and quietly, his voice nevertheless full of authority, he said "I think you must stay where you are, Myles. I need your help here. I am not asking you to do anything difficult, for I am convinced you will never find a more rewarding life than that which is yours already at Ellanbane. Do not despise your inheritance I beg of you." His tone was conciliatory and, looking into his face, I saw how much he was longing for me to say I would not leave him.

But I was determined to go. I shook my head and, with face averted, I told him my mind was made up. "I must go" I said ungraciously. "I must be free to live my life as I wish." There was a touch of irritation in my voice, and I knew I was handling things badly. For up to that moment he had not spoken a harsh word, but now his face grew flushed and angry. Stiffly he reminded me of all he had done for me. His whole manner changed from conciliation to downright denunciation. He was full of bitter reproach, impressing on me how disappointed my father would have been had he lived. He told me I was selfish and even accused me of cruelty, and the stony stare from his keen blue eyes nearly melted my resolve, but I was obstinate. I sat with lowered head looking at my feet. I had nothing more to say and longed for our *tête à tête* to end.

After a long silence during which the only sound in the room was that of the burning logs settling themselves in the grate, he gave a deep sigh and stared down at his empty glass. "Very well, my boy," he said dismissively. "You must do as you wish, but I believe you are making a grave mistake." His tone was constrained and a little weary. His eyes half closed.

I was so astounded at this quick turn-about that I sat for a moment or two rooted to my seat, unable to take it in. Then I reached over to shake his hand. "Thank you" I said fervently. "I am extremely grateful to you for letting me go, for to tell the truth I would find the move difficult to make without your consent. Once I have had a few years to see the world, I promise to come back and take up my duties again."

He smiled ruefully, and a few minutes later, as we stood up to leave, he said, his voice now gentle, "Although I hoped very much that you would agree to stay, nevertheless I wish you well," and I felt that, despite our disagreement and harsh words, we still had a great affection for one another.

Next morning at the breakfast table he was bright and amiable, still hoping I would reconsider my decision to leave. He asked me if my mind was fully made up, and I found him hard to resist, but I told him it was, and he did not press me any further. Instead, to my great joy, he told me he had been thinking things over, and although he was still sure I was wrong to go, he wanted me to have the best possible start in my new career. He promised me a gift of £500 before I left, and said he would use his influence with the Derby family to procure a commission for me. So, with a great lifting of the spirit, I set to work to put all in order before leaving the Island.

Between us we chose a new steward. He was Thomas Cleator, the second son of a Southside farmer, an energetic young fellow who seemed anxious to please, and I felt sure we had made an excellent choice.

The application for my commission went through without a hitch, and within weeks I heard I had been granted a lieutenancy in Her Majesty's Forces on the continent – a great honour for one so young. And now I had to set about saying my farewells: first of all to the Karrans at Castletown, then to George and Kitty and little Huan and last, but not least, to my dear dog Scamp and Peggy my mare, which caused me considerable heartache. Kitty, her eyes wet with tears, held me close when I bade her goodbye. She was the only mother I had ever known and there was great love between us.

"May God keep you safe and bring you home again soon" she said. She gave me a little Bollan cross "for luck", and I have kept it right up to this day.

On the morning I left, my grandfather and the two girls, Barbara and Rose, were waiting in the hall to see me on my way. Aunt Bella was in the carriage drawn up at the front door, ready to drive me and my luggage to Ramsey, where I was to board a cargo boat bound for Liverpool. In the midst of handshakes, good wishes and kisses all round, a curious thing happened. For, as I kissed Barbara I suddenly became aware that I loved her with more than cousinly love. She was smiling into my eyes, her handsome face aglow with tenderness as she gave me another kiss and a quick hug, and I resolved then and there to ask her to marry me when I came back again. Then Rose flung her arms about me. "Goodbye Myles" she said, adding, in a whisper disconcertingly loud enough for all to hear,

"I shall marry you when I am old enough. I love you very much." I was amused. I laughed and patted her shoulder gently. "We shall have to see about that" I said, and she blushed with pleasure. I was fond of her too. She was so shy and pretty, her big blue eyes full of affection, her golden curls encircling her head like a nimbus. Nevertheless, I knew without a shadow of doubt that Barbara was the girl for me.

My grandfather followed me to the carriage and, before I got in, he laid his hands on my shoulders. "I hope", he said reflectively, "that you will soon get over this desire for adventure. Your father was very little older than you when he married, and my dearest wish is to see you settled here with a wife and family before I die."

"I am quite sure you will" I said and, trying to console him, I took his hand and pressed it. A smile lit up his eyes for a moment, but he looked tired and disappointed. For the first time I wondered if I were doing the right thing. Ought I to be leaving him?

CHAPTER ELEVEN

It was about five in the afternoon when, after a journey much hampered by squally cross winds, we arrived at Liverpool. As I stepped ashore, a stiff north-easter was whistling across the cobbled landing place, so cold that I bent my head and drew the collar of my greatcoat high above my ears.

Feeling hungry as well as cold, not having eaten since leaving home that morning, I threaded my way through jostling crowds of stevedores unloading cargoes from tall ships lying at anchor in the port, hoping to find somewhere to stay nearby.

I was lucky to find an inn close to the waterfront where I had a hot meal and a room for the night. I was also able to buy a useful horse at the adjoining stable-yard, which I would re-sell at my journey's end. So, next morning after an early breakfast, I rode off through narrow dockside lanes, out across the flat Lancashire countryside and into a hinterland of heathland and woods, notoriously the hideout of footpads and cut-throats. Fortunately, I encountered none of these dangerous gentlemen, save those hanging from creaking gibbets, no longer able to pursue their nefarious calling.

After a few overnight stops at uncomfortable hostelries which offered only poor food and flea-ridden beds, I came with pleasure to the soft, beautiful counties of southern England.

A day or two later I arrived at the headquarters of the Honourable Artillery Company of London where I was to receive my military education. I found the training there rough and harsh. Raw recruits like myself had to be made into competent fighting men in the least possible time, seeing that a bitter war was at present raging between Spain and Holland and, as Spain had for many years been an enemy of England, our armed forces were regularly giving great assistance to the Dutch.

So it was that, only three gruelling weeks after my arrival at headquarters, I boarded a naval vessel at Greenwich fully prepared to take command of two hundred men under my captain's orders.

The struggle was now centred at Ostend, a small town of low thatched houses and barely 3,000 inhabitants. It was the only piece of land in Flanders possessed by the Dutch, but the Archduke Albert was determined to acquire it, encouraged by his wife Isabella whose father had bequeathed it to her without the slightest right to do so.

Queen Elizabeth of England was just as resolute that he should not succeed, and promised Maurice of Nassau 5,000 men to assist him in defending the town. Many young men of good family had volunteered for service, having learned their drill as citizens in the militia, a course of action unfortunately not available in the Isle of Man.

However, the main body of the troops was drawn from London prisons, the flotsam and jetsam of the towns, and from poor creatures caught by impressment officers. Indeed I was filled with dismay on arrival at Ostend when I saw the motley crew put into my charge, and they proved beyond doubt to be an unruly bunch. Looting and rioting were habitual amongst them, and drunkenness too when they could get hold of sufficient liquor. But, with stern discipline and a certain amount of rough justice, the ruffian elements were gradually licked into shape.

The hostilities turned out to be fierce and bitter, with neither side showing much initial gain. Owing to the control of the seaboard being in the hands of the Dutch, they were able to import men and provisions *ad lib*, and on the enemy's side also there was no lack of men, food, guns and ammunition, and, as soon as the ranks at any time grew thin, more Spaniards and Italians promptly appeared on the field to earn their five stivers a day, and a grave in the trenches.

Our own commander-in-chief, Sir Francis Vere, was well skilled in the art of war. He knew how to use his men to the best advantage and, together with his most trusty and daring officers, wiped out company after company of the Archduke's men by cleverly contrived surprises.

Unfortunately, during one of these sorties, the captain of my company was smashed by a canon ball and dropped dead at my feet. Thereupon, I had to take instant command, and was abruptly promoted from lieutenant to captain on the spot.

On that same day, one of my men, a brave young Cornishman, John Carew, lost an arm. It had been carried some distance away, but courageously he picked it up and brought it to the field surgeon crying "Behold the arm which today at dinner served my whole body." Likewise, the majority of our men were splendid soldiers, and showed great courage, but the work of defence was becoming ever more grim, for we were cursed with several spies within our ranks who were drawing substantial pay from the enemy, one of whom, a fellow named Coningsby, was daily supplying information to them on our plans of campaign.

He had also prepared a plot for blowing up a magazine, thus opening up a gap sufficient to allow the Duke's men to scramble through and attack at close quarters. Fortunately for us, he was unable to carry out his stratagem single-handed, for he confided his scheme to a sergeant, who went to the Governor with the information, and Master Coningsby was consigned to the rack and dungeon.

But now we were faced with yet another hazard, as the sea began to make great inroads on our flanking outworks, and our gruesome task was constantly to make a wall of corpses to shut out the water. We collected all bodies lying around, and even disinterred others from their rest to add to the putrid mass of flesh and bones.

As was to be expected, pestilence broke out and our troops were decimated. Our troubles deepened when, with sad hearts, we learned of the death of our beloved Queen Elizabeth, and we were uncertain whether or not the war would continue, but the sad news altered nothing. Men and provisions continued to come in shiploads by order of the new monarch, King James, and the hostilities could have lasted for many more years if only our fortifications had held. Unhappily they were becoming old and unstable. One by one, they were collapsing under the onslaught of forty-pounders and massive bombardment from storming parties. The Italians and Walloons were advancing inexorably until, at last, only one riddled and shaky fort remained. Then, suddenly and for no obvious reason, just as defeat seemed inevitable, a parley was sounded and, after a great deal of talk and negotiating, the siege of Ostend ended with a twelve year truce.

By this time, I was becoming a little disillusioned with warfare. All in all, I decided the siege had been futile. I grieved for the loss of so many brave companions, especially as there was nothing at all to show for their sacrifice. Full of bitterness and disappointment, I watched as the Spaniards proudly took possession of a riddled fort, a little powder, a heap of ruins and the sepulchre of 140,000 men.

CHAPTER TWELVE

After the fall of Ostend, I was draughted with a portion of the troops, first to Sluys, then to Leyden, where I was engaged solely in garrison duty.

Leyden, I discovered, was a lovely dignified old town, of gently flowing canals spanned by elegant bridges; and I was fascinated by the medieval charm of its narrow shopping lanes and ancient alleyways. In every street looms clacked, and whirred, from dawn until dusk, since it was the universal hub of the textile trade, where even the English sent their prime cloth to be finished.

It was also a cultural centre. Its university, though small and consisting of only two colleges, was fast becoming famous for its brilliant scholarship. So, having a good deal of spare time from my military duties, I embarked on a course of study there, with the intention of improving my knowledge of modern languages.

Going to and fro between garrison and university, I often met a soberly dressed young man, a few years older than myself. He was dark haired and handsome, and had fine intelligent eyes. For some reason he interested me as soon as I saw him, and I was pleased when one day he stopped to speak. He was, he told me, doing religious studies, and suggested I attend some of the debates in his faculty. He assured me they were both informative and very lively, and he thought I would enjoy them. He was so persuasive that, when time allowed, I went to listen to these debates in which he generally took a major part. He had a sharp, well-informed and logical mind, and often had the best of it even against the most learned professors. The arguments were as a rule between the Calvinists, with their depressing theory of predestination, and the more joyful Armenians, who held that all mankind could earn salvation through repentance. His name was John Robinson, and he was pastor of a local church established and maintained by exiles from England called Separatists. They were, he explained, as we were strolling together one day through the University gardens, a group of people that had been much persecuted because of their objections to some of the ceremonious practices in the Church of England. They had refused to attend church services, meeting instead in their own homes for worship. For this misdemeanor severe laws were passed against them. Many of their number had been imprisoned, many more heavily fined and some had even been put to death.

At once my sympathy was aroused and I spoke at some length on how wrong I considered any form of religious persecution to be. At the same time I was thinking not only of Mr McAuley and the tragic victimisation of Catholics in England

49

but also of the horrors of St Bartholomew's day in Paris, and I was remembering too the charnel house I had just left at Ostend, which had largely been the end result of a religious war begun forty years ago in the Netherlands.

As he listened, I saw him glance at me speculatively once or twice, his eyes keen and acute. Then, when I had finished speaking, he turned to me and, with an expression of extreme gentleness, he said "I am glad to hear your views, Myles, for they accord in every respect with my own." Gradually, a warm friendship developed between us and some time later he invited me to his home, Groenepoort (Green Gate), a large house which served as Meeting House and Parsonage, where I met his wife, Bridget, a gentle quietly spoken woman and his three fine children, John, Bridget and Isaac. On subsequent visits there, I met several leaders and members of the Church. They were all intelligent men, pleasant and easy to talk to, with whom I formed a cordial relationship and, when John Robinson suggested that I attend one of the services at Pieterskerk, I was happy to agree.

The meetings were held twice on Sundays: in the morning from 8 o'clock until noon and in the afternoon from 2 o'clock until five or six. I went in the morning and found it to be a novel experience. The Meeting House was quite large and smelled oddly of pitchpine and varnish. It was packed to overflowing with shiny-faced, devout worshippers who sat with open bibles on their knees ready to follow the scriptural readings, the men sitting on wooden benches to one side and the women apart across the aisle. The sum total of the Separatists in Leyden were 473 men, women and children, all living in a little network of streets close to their church and it appeared that most of them were present on this particular morning. The service began with a long extempore prayer, which was punctuated by ecstatic Amens and Halleluyahs from the congregation who did not kneel, but stood, for kneeling they thought an idolatrous practise. Then several members, one after another, read a chapter from the Bible and discussed its content at great length. Next a preacher gave out a text and preached on it in a flat monotonous voice for over an hour. He was followed by several more speakers. This made the meeting inordinately long and, with the exception of a sermon by John Robinson, it was both prosaic and boring. Psalms were sung without instrumental music of any kind, all lifting their voices together after a deacon set the pitch. The singing I thought was particularly bad.

I had great sympathy for the many young children in the congregation. They were herded together in a long pew at the front of the church, shepherded by a grim looking deaconess with a sallow, melancholy face and gimlet eyes. She had a birch rod conveniently placed at her side, ready to use on any child that grew restive. I watched with a feeling of repugnance as she kept twisting her head, ever at the alert for any sign of misbehaviour, which she immediately punished with a swish of the birch.

At the end of the meeting, I spoke to John Bradford, one of the elders of the Church that I met at the Robinson's house, and told him I considered it a great pity to terrify youngsters in this way. He merely shrugged his shoulders and said, beaming at me blandly,"Our deaconess is a fine Christian and an ornament to the congregation." As he spoke, I was thinking how fortunate it was for me as a child, that the little church at home in Lezayre had no such ornament. This harshness was one of the less admirable traits of the Separatists, one which I found hard to understand for, in the main, they were a loving and compassionate community.

Soon after that first meeting, John Robinson began pressing me to join them but, much as I admired them for their goodness and sincerity, I declined. Even had I been a practising Christian, which indeed I was not, I would not have wished to be committed to any particular sect. To me, it seems a tragedy that men's worst passions are excited because of their different ways of worshipping God. Nevertheless I was grateful to these people for the kindness and warm friendship they had shown me, and which I am thankful to say I never lost.

On the completion of a full year's duty at Leyden I was beginning to feel restless. I had been a soldier now for seven years – long, hard, monotonous years they had been, in which I had experienced none of the excitement and challenge I had hoped for. Consequently, I was beginning to feel it was time to redeem my promise to my grandfather to return home when I was tired of roving. In his letters, he never failed to remind me that I had been away long enough, and that he needed me at Ellanbane. We had, during all this time, been able to keep up a fairly lively correspondence, even though we were so many miles apart. This was because of our relationship with the Derby family, who had the privilege of using the royal couriers in recognition of services rendered to the Crown. Accordingly, our letters travelled safely and swiftly under their insignia.

However, as it was several months since I had last heard from him, I was growing a little anxious. He was by now a very old man, and might be ill or even dead, so, all things considered, I decided to see my commanding officer and ask for a few weeks leave of absence. I thought it better to postpone resigning my commission until I returned to duty with my future plans cut and dried. As it turned out, it was most fortunate that I left things in abeyance at this juncture. My request granted, I bade my Separatist friends goodbye and set off as soon as I could for London, on the first leg of my journey home.

It was a wonderful feeling to set foot on English soil again after such a long absence, but London itself depressed me. It was as usual full of life and jollity, the great heart and brain of England, but at every turn I came across men that had been under my command at Ostend. They were poverty stricken and haunting the streets hopelessly, some of them minus an eye or an arm, or limping pitifully on one leg. Many of them were either begging for their bread or pilfering from local tradesmen. As a result they were ignominiously hauled back to the jails from which they had enlisted. This then was the "Glory" they had fought for, and I felt sick at heart.

More than ever, I wanted to get back to the peaceful life waiting for me in the Isle of Man. My first concern, therefore, was to invest in a stout horse for the journey northwards, and I had taken lodgings in an inn near Fleet Street while I looked for a suitable mount. So next day, on a bright and sunny morning, soon after breakfast, I was walking down Cheapside on my way to the stables of a

51

dealer that had been highly recommended by the innkeeper. I had just turned into a side street leading to the stables when a miserable looking creature ambled towards me, holding out a shaking hand on which only two fingers remained. He was trembling as if from the ague. "Please spare a copper for a wounded soldier" he whined. I dropped a coin or two into his palm and was about to move on when the fellow gazed hard into my face and, with a look of dawning recognition, caught hold of my sleeve. "Young Myles Standish I'll be bound" he exclaimed. "Do you remember me, Jacques the Frenchman?"

I stared back at him. He was far removed from the handsome young rake I had known. His face was grey and lantern-jawed, a little sinister too, with sunken temples and a beaky nose that almost met his chin. Yet, for all that, I recognised him by his snapping black eyes, the one feature which seldom changes except perhaps to grow a little less acute. "Yes I remember you", I said, not very pleased to see him for I had never liked the man, "but kindly excuse me as I have some urgent business to attend to."

He looked at me with a regretful, embarrassed smile, and spoke with a warmth that was full of longing. "Please spare me a little of your time, Myles," he pleaded. "I know in the past I have been a wicked lout with nothing at all to commend me. But I long to hear something of the people I knew in the Isle of Man, when I was in my prime, and before I went to the wars and ended up the wreck you see before you."

As he floundered through his speech, I was moved to pity, and a little ashamed of wanting to give him the cold shoulder. "Come on then," I said, "we will drink a tankard of ale apiece, and talk of old times together". His face lit up with pleasure as I took his arm and led him to a nearby ale house. It was a cheerful, busy place, with a blazing log fire and an appetizing smell of cooking. We sat at a table in a corner and I ordered a plate of veal and ham pie and a jug of ale for us both. Jacques was obviously starving, for he ate avidly, concentrating on his food without either looking up from his plate or uttering a word. He had polished off the meal before I had properly started on mine, so I ordered another serving for him. This time he munched away a little less quickly, stopping now and again to ask about various friends of his in Lezayre and the farmers he had worked for: then of Voirrey, and Kitty, and George Quayle.

He looked a little rueful on hearing that old Mylecraine had died, and that Voirrey had since married, but nodded sagely over Kitty and George's wedded bliss. "Those two were made for each other" he said with a sly grin. "Voirrey and I would have done well together too", he went on, "but, when the old man cut her out of his will, I knew I could never have kept her in comfort, so I made myself scarce."

"Not before you nearly scotched things for Kitty and George though" I put in.

He shrugged his shoulders and glanced at me archly from under thick bushy eyebrows. "I know I did wrong", he said with a touch of his old bravado, "but I was young and foolish and, after all, it has apparently worked out well in the end." Then, with head thrown back, he gave an impudent chuckle: "I had a lot of fun with the girls in those days" he said. His black eyes were glinting rakishly, and it was plain to see that the "old Adam" was not quite dead within him, even yet. I had no more news to give him as I had been a long time away from home myself, and there was a copious silence between us.

Then suddenly he leaned towards me, his face close to mine, and with a quick gesture felt inside his coat pocket. "Look here" he said, and dangled a silver object in front of my eyes. It glistened and shone in the firelight.

I held out my hand and took it, sure that I had seen it before. I turned it over a time or two. "The Mylecraine Cross" I exclaimed. "How did you come by it?"

His face darkened. "I stole it from under the old fellow's nose" he said. "He always hated me, and I took it more from spite than anything else. I have often been tempted to sell it, especially when I have been hungry and penniless, but somehow I could never bring myself to part with it. But now I would like you to take it to Voirrey. Please tell her I have never forgotten her, and I wish her well." His voice broke a little, and tears were starting in his eyes.

"I will see that Voirrey gets it. Kitty will send it on and give her your message as well" I said, as I put it carefully away in an inside pocket of my greatcoat.

Then we talked a little of our wartime experiences. He told me that he had been badly wounded several times. Once in the stomach, and also in the shoulder and hand. I was amazed that, although we had served in the same field of battle, we had at no time met. Finally, I asked him how he proposed to live in the future, for I was pretty sure he was quite destitute.

He did not answer for a moment or two. Then he drained his jug of ale judiciously, and gazed at me with a doubtful expression. "I have been hoping to find a berth on one of the cargo boats sailing between Dover and France. I have cousins in Le Havre with a large bakery business, and I have good reason to believe they will give me employment. Unfortunately, I have not the wherewithal to travel even as far as Dover, let alone France, for a thieving fellow robbed me of all I possessed two days ago.

I reached into my pocket, and handed him five gold sovereigns. "This will take you to France and also keep you for a time until you are settled in Le Havre" I said gently.

In silence, he pocketed the money. Then, with a radiant smile, "Thank you Myles" he said. "I do not deserve such kindness, but I am truly grateful and my problem is solved. I hope some day to repay you."

"Think nothing of it" I said: "it is a gift, a thank offering to Fate for my own health and strength."

Soon afterwards we left and strolled back together to the stables, where we shook hands and parted. Sadly I watched him walk away with the faltering steps of an old man. He had gone such a long way down-hill since I had last seen him that I found it difficult even to conjure up a picture of the old devil-may-care Jacques. "*Sic transit gloria mundi*" I murmured as he disappeared into the distance.

CHAPTER THIRTEEN

An hour later, after some hard bargaining, I had bought a useful mare, and very early next morning was in the saddle bound for the north-west. I travelled light, with only the minimum of requirements packed into a saddle bag, and before noon the cobbled streets of London lay far behind me. There was but one thought in my mind now and that was to get home as quickly as possible. So, after each overnight stay in various indifferent wayside taverns, I arose at dawn and took to the road again with all speed. In this way I made good time and, in less than two weeks, arrived at Ormskirk in Lancashire on a cold November evening, both saddle-sore and weary.

I found a lodging for the night at the Snigs Foot in the High Street, where I had excellent service. A groom looked after my horse, who was as tired as I was, and led her away to the stables while the landlord himself showed me to my room, then sent a servant girl along with a ewer of hot water. After I had washed and made myself presentable, I went in search of something to eat. A pot boy directed me to a room directly behind the bar-parlour. Inside the vista was warm and welcoming. It was empty as I entered: the candles were not yet lit, but a crackling log fire set shadows dancing on the walls, and shone on a long table of gleaming oak, already spread for a meal. Before long the pot-boy arrived with candles, and the information that supper would soon be served. So I drew up a chair, and settled myself at table. Gradually the room began to fill up with wayfarers like myself. There must have been between twenty and thirty people all told, and soon everyone was talking amiably across the crowded table, meanwhile tucking into a splendid meal of boiled beef, vegetables and savoury dumplings, all washed down with hot spiced home-brewed ale.

Then the landlord brought in two latecomers, and beckoned the serving-maid to lay a couple more places. They sat down at the far end of the table, where their faces were in shadow, but when the elder of the two bade the company "Good Evening" before starting his supper, I thought his clear rich voice sounded familiar. I scrutinised him more closely, and with a rush of surprise saw he was my old friend and mentor, Father McAuley. I leaned forward, gave a little cough to attract his attention, and caught his eye. He gazed straight at me for a moment or two, his face transfixed with a mixture of astonishment and consternation. Then he stiffened warily, but gave no answering sign of recognition. He leaned back in his chair, one hand resting on the table, and, without another glance in my direction, began talking earnestly to his companion who listened with inclined head and an occasional nod.

He was a young man of about my age, slim and goodlooking. His finely boned face appeared strained and tense, and his eyes had a quality of sadness in them that somehow gave the impression of innate goodness. I felt a little mortified at being ignored like this and, although I realised they had good reason to be secretive, I was a little on edge and, as soon as I had finished eating, I left the table as unobtrusively as possible and went up to my room.

It was too early to go to bed, so I sat before an empty grate reading a little book on farming I had bought in London. But, before I had turned the first page, there was a discreet knock on the door. I opened it to the landlord, who asked me to accompany him to a private room below, where two gentlemen wished to speak to me. It was easy to guess who the two men were and, at the foot of the stairs, he ushered me through a door which opened into a small room with whitewashed walls and a low oak-beamed ceiling. Several rushlight candles were burning brightly on the mantelshelf over a comfortable fire, and Father McAuley and his friend were sitting before it on a long wooden settle.

They looked up, smiling affably, as I entered, and Father McAuley leapt to his feet and, coming towards me with arms outstretched, embraced me. Then, drawing me towards the settle, he introduced me to his friend, Edmund Arrowsmith. As we sat down together, he said "It was impolite of me not to recognise you at the supper table, but these are anxious days, Myles, and there are spies everywhere. The landlord here is a good Catholic, and we make his house our headquarters when we are in the vicinity. He puts it about that we are itinerant artists visiting the great houses in the neighbourhood in order to paint portraits of the family. However, quite apart from the need for secrecy, I was also badly shaken when I saw you sitting there alive and well, for I had heard you were killed at Ostend some months ago." Suddenly his eyes grew sad, his expression grave and unsmiling. He got up and leaned his back wearily against the mantelshelf. Turning full on me, he gave me a piercing look and raised his voice: "Why have you not written to your grandfather during the last ten months?" he asked.

I stared up at him mystified. "But I have written to him regularly all the time I have been away", I cried, "and have had no reply to my letters for a very long time. That is why I am here to-night, for I am on my way home to see if all is well with him." Then suddenly a thought occurred to me. "Who told you I had died?" I asked.

As I waited for an answer, he looked at me with a troubled, thoughtful gaze and, after a short silence, said gently "As you know, Myles, it became impossible for me to show my face at Ellanbane after my last unfortunate visit, but for some years now another priest has travelled to the Isle of Man at intervals to administer to the needs of the Catholic community there. Naturally, as his confessor, he came to know your grandfather well, and gave me news of him from time to time. The story goes that your Cousin William, while on a visit to London, met a soldier from your regiment who declared he had seen you felled by a bullet which killed you instantly. This dreadful information, I might tell you, broke your grandfather's heart." He paused for a moment, then, clearing his throat, his face working with emotion, he went on: "Prepare yourself for bad news Myles, for I have to tell you that your grandfather breathed his last, two months ago. He died with your name on his lips!"

I gave a wild cry, and sat for a long time staring wordlessly into space. The room seemed to close in on me and I felt numb. Remorse and guilt were gnawing away inside me. At this moment I realised how selfish I had been to leave home, how cruel to ignore my grandfather's pleadings to return, and now I should never see him again. After a while I began to question Father McAuley. "Have you any idea why our letters were not delivered?" I asked. "Have there been any great storms that prevented communication with the Island, or any shipping disasters?"

He considered, stroking his chin with his forefinger. "No," he said, "I cannot recall any such calamities. All I know is that for many months before your grandfather's death he had no word from you. He was quite convinced that you were dead, so much so that, apart from some minor bequests to the two girls, Rose and Barbara, and their mother, Mrs Standish, he has left his entire estate to your Cousin William."

"What" I cried. "Are you now telling me that my birthright has also gone?"

He nodded gravely. "I am afraid so" he said, "and that same William has become an intolerable worry to me, a great thorn in the flesh. For, to please your grandfather, he became a Catholic shortly after you left home, but since that good man's death he has renounced the Faith and taken himself off to live at the Court of King James. By all accounts he cuts a great dash there, and is a firm favourite amongst all of London's high society. My anxiety stems from the fact that he is well aware of the present hide-outs of many of our seminaries and knows the name of every recusant in the north of England." Suddenly his voice was harsh and angry. "I have indisputable evidence", he said, "that William has been instrumental in bringing several of our people to a horrible death on the gallows." He passed a hand across his eyes as if to shut out painful memories. Then he looked at me, bewildered and wretched. "I hate to say this, Myles, but William has become a thoroughly evil man."

I thought back quickly. "He has been evil for as long as I have known him, Father," I said. I remembered how he had persecuted me at school: I felt again the anguish he had caused me with his biting sarcasm, and the physical pain I had endured through his skulduggery. There was a long silence, then suddenly we gazed at one another, both struck with the same thought. All at once it seemed obvious that Willian had had a hand in intercepting the letters.

I said as much to Father McAuley and he, frowning and nodding his head gloomily, agreed that the possibility had just occurred to him too. "But you will never be able to prove it" he said. "Be very sure I will do my utmost" I replied. But somehow just then I did not feel nearly so outraged at losing my inheritance as I became some time later. The loss of my grandfather filled my mind to the exclusion of all else and my·heart was rent.

56

During the whole time Father McAuley and I had been talking, Edmund Arrowsmith had been glancing at me with eyes full of concern. Suddenly he leaned forward and, placing a firm hand on my shoulder, kept it there in mute sympathy. "I am deeply sorry for you in your trouble", he said in a quiet agreeable voice, "and nothing I can say is going to help. Only God Himself can give you comfort. But think how much harder bereavement must be for unbelievers than for Christians. We are so blest in having the sure and certain hope of meeting our loved ones again. How lucky we are. Do you not agree?" He spoke so calmly and intimately, so certain that I too was a Christian, that I had not the heart to disabuse him. "Surely you realise", he went on, "that, at your grandfather's great age, he had come to the end of his life, and it was better to slip gently away as he did?"

I stiffened. "I know all that", I said bitterly, "but I feel I hastened his end, and it grieves me that I was not there to bid him Goodbye. Also I am concerned that he went so sadly, believing me to have died." After this outburst, nothing further was said on the matter, but I was comforted and supported by the presence of these two good men. They were determined to keep me from brooding, and to see me through the night.

As we sat, Edmund told me a little of his background. He was almost exactly my own age. He had been born at Haydock, educated at Douai in France, ordained a priest in the Jesuit Order and had, for some time now, accompanied Father McAuley on his dangerous missions up and down the country. For himself, he seemed to be oblivious to the perils and hazards of his life and, as he spoke, I felt he had great qualities, an intelligence that would have taken him far in any profession he cared to choose, and I began to admire him tremendously.

At last the fire burned low in the grate, and the room grew cold, so reluctantly we bade one another Goodnight and went off to bed. But I could not sleep. I lay there encompassed with misery. I wanted to pray but was not able. I could not even weep. At about five o'clock I got up and drew back the curtains. It was black dark outside, but there was a shaft of uneven intermittent light coming from the inn doorway directly below my window. Presently I saw two figures emerge, one carrying a lantern and large knapsack, the other a painter's easel. I watched as they stumped purposefully up the High Street to disappear at last into the night.

Alas I never saw either of them again, for a few years later, eleven to be precise, when I was thousands of miles away and in another continent, I learned with great sadness that they were both dead. Edmund Arrowsmith had been captured near Brindle and taken to Lancaster Castle. There, after a mockery of a trial, he was hanged, drawn and quartered. A year later Father McAuley suffered the same fate in a market town near Leicester.

It was still dark but, feeling restless and despondent, I went downstairs, breakfasted by candles and at first light rode across to Lathom House, the home of the Earls of Derby. This was a splendid mansion lying back in acres of land surrounded by trees in the village of Knowsley, barely six miles from Ormskirk.

I was hoping to find the present Earl in residence as I needed his help in discovering for certain by whom my letters had been intercepted. It was beginning to dawn on me how much the loss of my inheritance would alter my whole life, and I had it in mind to take the case to law. I was in luck's way for, when I arrived at Lathom House, the great nail-studded front door was opened to my knock by a stately major-domo who informed me that the Earl was at breakfast. "Please tell him", I said, "that Captain Myles Standish wishes to have a word with him."

Within minutes I was ushered into a vast dining room with a marble floor and splendid painted ceiling. The Earl was just finishing his meal at a long table that stretched almost the full length of the room. Wiping his lips with a napkin, he rose and came towards me with outstretched hand to greet me. He was a powerfully built man, tall with a handsome head and a pair of prominent blue eyes beneath a somewhat low brow. I had met him only once before, on a rare occasion when he had dined at Ellanbane, for he seldom visited the Isle of Man, and took no interest in it. But his wife lived there and so did his son, Lord Strange, whom I knew tolerably well.

"Sit down, Captain Myles," he said, pulling out a dining chair from the table. Then, with both hands in his pockets and towering over me, he eyed me closely. "I was profoundly sorry to learn of the death of your grandfather" he said. "He was a man I liked, and esteemed, but little did I think to see you here this morning, for I had heard you had also died in Holland during the siege of Ostend. I understand young William Standish is now heir to all your grandfather's properties."

Looking up at him, and seeing his eyes sparkling with inquisitiveness, I began at once to explain how it was I had been presumed dead, due in no small measure to the non-arrival of my letters. In some curious way, telling him of my troubles, my changed circumstances and the shock and remorse I felt over my grandfather's death seemed to bring me comfort. He listened intently, standing there before me like a commander-in-chief. By the time I had finished my tale of woe, his face had flushed an angry purple. Abruptly he strode to the door, opened it and, with a mighty bellow, demanded that the courier be brought to him. Seconds later the fellow arrived, and he began firing questions at him. "Did he remember delivering the letters to Ellanbane?"

"Yes indeed, my lord. I have taken letters there for several years."

"And did you collect any to be delivered to Captain Myles Standish?"

"Not since more than a twelvemonth gone" he said.

"Who took delivery of the letters at Ellanbane?"

"A tall, plump young gentleman, my lord," and then he went on to describe Cousin William to the life.

I felt my gorge rise, but kept my anger to myself. I thanked the fellow for his information which served to confirm my suspicions of William's guilt.

When he had left the room, Lord Derby came and laid an arm about my shoulders, half turning towards me, and in a quiet sincere voice said gently "I am very sorry to have to remind you that the odds are against you. It will be impossible to have your grandfather's will revoked on the evidence of one man's word alone. The whole affair is too complicated and your cousin will find it easy to lie himself out of trouble."

"I am sure you are right, sir," I said, touched by his sympathy, "and I am truly grateful for your kindness, but I intend to try."

He made no further comment except to add that I would always be welcome in his house. We shook hands warmly and, before long, I was on my way to the Liverpool docks. I was on tenterhooks to get home. I wanted to find out how things were going on now that William was the Master, albeit an absent one. I still had a forlorn hope that a place would be found for me there and that some settlement could be made, once it was established that the news of my death had been an ill-founded rumour.

I sold my horse at the livery stables near the waterfront and took passage on a brig bound for Castletown with a load of timber. We weighed anchor just before eleven o'clock, and were on the open sea within the hour. The old familiar tang of salt was on my lips, and I was full of pleasure at the thought that I would soon be on my native soil again.

Unfortunately, after we had been on our way for upwards of three hours, a severe gale blew up which hampered our progress. Strong winds whistled through the rigging and swept over the deck. One mammoth sea smashed into the ship and put her beam under water, and I began to fear for our safety. I was sure she would sink, but gradually the storm abated and, after having been pitched about for two days on a voyage that usually took about twelve hours with a following wind, we arrived at Castletown on a mild and sunny day in early December.

CHAPTER FOURTEEN

The little grey town was, as usual, wrapped in quiet dignity. Nothing had visibly changed since I was last here – the great castle towering majestically over a huddle of limestone houses, the little boats swaying peacefully at anchor in the harbour, flocks of gulls whining angrily overhead. It was almost as if time had been standing still.

A small crowd had gathered to watch as we tied up alongside a flight of seaweed-covered steps, and I was surprised when a voice greeted me by name from somewhere amongst it. I looked up and recognised the cheerful, smiling face of Joe Karran.

As quickly as possible, I made my farewells to the skipper and crew of the brig, floundered up the green oozy steps and gripped his hand. He had broadened and thickened into a muscular, splendidly built young man, tall and straight as a die. "It is good to see you, Joe," I cried, slipping into the vernacular easily, just as if I had never been away.

As we shook hands, he was gazing into my eyes with gentle concern. "We heard you had gone from us for good" he said, "but somehow I never believed it, for only the good die young, eh Myles?" Grinning broadly, he dug his fist gleefully into my chest a time or two, then clapped me on the shoulder in a gesture of friendship, and I found his affectionate welcome oddly gratifying. "Father will be overjoyed to see you" he said as we walked alongside the old ramparts of the castle, but before turning into Parliament Lane I told him I had first of all to visit the livery stables to hire a mount for my journey home.

"There is no need for that", said Joe, "for Father and I have bought a small croft on the Malew road, where we keep six milch cows and a work horse. In this way we can make a few pounds when the fishing is poor. The horse is a bit on the heavy side, but good enough to take you home and you can ride pillion if you like. I would be glad enough to have a trip north." Then, turning to me with a shy, embarrassed smile, he announced that he was soon to be married to a Ramsey girl. Her name was Islen Faragher, and he had met her earlier in the year at Maughold Fair. His father liked her, and he felt sure they would, all three of them, get on well together. "It will be grand", he said, "to have a woman in the house again, to cook and wash, and keep everything ship-shape." But although his words sounded matter of fact and lacking in emotion, his expression had softened, a certain pride shone through and I knew him well enough to be sure he loved his Islen deeply.

We found his father sitting before a glowing turf fire, mending a pile of nets, in the cluttered, fishy-smelling living room of the little cottage. His welcome was as heart-warming as Joe's had been. As soon as he saw me, he leapt to his feet, nimble as ever, and looking only slightly older than when I saw him last, even though his hair was now completely white and his eyes surrounded by a network of tiny wrinkles. He grasped both my hands in his, and gave a great triumphant shout.

"I am uncommonly glad to see you, Myles" he cried. "I was absolutely certain you would turn up again some time or other, and here you are sound in wind and limb." Our eyes met, and I felt sure that, in some curious way, both Joe and he had known I was still alive. This puzzled me, and some time later, as we sat to a traditional Manx meal of salt herrings, potatoes and buttermilk that Joe had prepared, I asked them how they had come to this conclusion.

Joe regarded me benevolently, and gave a knowing wink: "Islen has a cousin who was for some time a maid-servant at Ellanbane", he said, "and she told Islen that letters were arriving from Holland months after you had been presumed killed there. Mr William Standish, she said, had given orders that he was to be called to take delivery whenever letters arrived for your grandfather, who had taken to his bed soon after the news of your death. She declared she had heard the courier on several occasions call out 'Despatch from Captain Myles Standish, sir,' on presenting the mail. So naturally we were pretty sure you were still alive, and that there was some skulduggery afoot, especially when we heard that your Cousin William had stepped so conveniently into your shoes."

I leaned forward eagerly. "You have guessed correctly" I said, "and now I must see this cousin of Islen. She might be a useful witness, when I contest my grandfather's will."

But Edward was shaking his head, and smiling obliquely. "She has since left the Island to keep house for William Standish in his new London home" he said, and for an instant I caught a lively salacious sparkle in his eye as he added "Your Cousin William, I am told, has an eye for the ladies, and she is a fine buxom girl".

I scowled in frustration and disgust, realising at once, as he meant me to, that I could expect no co-operation from that quarter. When we had finished the meal, we sat around the table for a while, gossiping about people I had known in the town, and I was saddened to learn that during the past year Mr and Mrs Christian of Knockrushen had died within weeks of one another. Mr Clucas, they told me, was still spry, but had retired from teaching, and there was another master at the grammar school.

But while we were talking I noticed a certain constraint in the air. Edward's face now showed signs of anxiety as he glanced at me sharply now and again, then looked away quickly. He was worried and uncomfortable. Eventually he fell silent, and I felt a spasm of unease. "Is something troubling you, Edward?" I asked at last.

He looked straight at me, flustered and full of disquiet, then turned to Joe: "I think you had better tell Myles the latest bad news – he will have it soon enough in any case" he said, and both their faces were strained as Joe, speaking quickly, and with obvious distress, told me that, just a fortnight before, Mrs Isabella Standish had met with a riding accident when crossing a narrow path leading to a neighbour's house. Her horse had stumbled, she had been thrown into a stone wall and had died instantly.

I gazed at Joe, stupified with shock, lost for words at this latest blow and on the verge of tears, for I had been fond of Aunt Bella. I stared steadily ahead, for I did not want to meet their sympathetic eyes. After a long silence I recovered myself. "I must get home at once", I said, "for Rose and Barbara will be out of their minds with grief, and I must go to them".

But Edward was frowning. "I think you had better stay here tonight", he said gently, "and set off in the morning when you can arrive before nightfall."

I paused for a moment, for his suggestion was practical. Already dusk was gathering even though it had only just turned three o'clock, and by the time I reached my destination the household would have retired for the night. So, reluctantly, I agreed to stay. But in the little attic bedroom under the eaves I lay awake for hours, my mind in a ferment, thinking about Rose and Barbara, worrying about their future and what it held for them. I had intended to ask Barbara to marry me when I returned home. I knew she was still free, because each of my grandfather's letters had included little messages from both young women, giving any titbits of local news that he had omitted. But now I realized I had no place at Ellanbane: I must therefore return to Holland soon to take up my military duties again, and I did not care to contemplate taking Barbara with me, so leaving Rose on her own.

CHAPTER FIFTEEN

Early next morning Joe and I set off on the big farm horse, I riding pillion. It was a dark, dank, misty morning, the hills invisible under a lowering grey sky and it was bitterly cold. I was a poor travelling companion, invaded with dread of the sad meeting at the end of the journey, and my conversation was forced. But Joe seemed not to notice. He laughed and cracked jokes, and rattled on contentedly about Islen and their plans for the future. He was supremely happy, and I was glad for him, nevertheless with just a touch of envy, for secretly I craved for a pleasant love like his. We rode along at a leisurely pace, and it was past noon before we came to the little village of St John's where we had some refreshment at a wayside eating house. Then, after giving the horse a feed of oats and a drink, we took to the road again, and arrived at the entrance to Ellanbane in late afternoon. I dismounted and, with a firm promise to visit him and his father again soon, left Joe to continue his journey to Ramsey, and walked slowly down the empty avenue. The stark, leafless trees on either side, jet black under a leaden sky, added to the melancholy of the day.

As I turned into the wide semi-circular driveway immediately before the house, unexpectedly the front door flew open and Barbara, white-faced and anxious, came running towards me. "We caught sight of you through the drawing room window" she cried. "Rose thought you were a ghost, and has collapsed in a dead faint. Come quickly, Myles! Come quickly!" She grasped my arm and together we ran through the hall into the drawing room.

Rose was lying on the floor, pale and still. I knelt beside her, raised her head gently and spoke her name. As I did so, her eyes flickered open, and some colour returned to the small white face. She gazed up at me, her eyes filled with wonder, and, putting up her hand, she stroked my face. "We thought you were dead" she murmured. Placing her arms around my shoulders, she raised herself to kiss me, then nestled her head under my chin with a contented sigh.

Barbara was smiling down at us, full of relief at Rose's quick recovery, and, as I looked up into the steady eyes in the mature handsome face, my heart quickened, a wave of love for her swept over me and I longed to take her in my arms. Her eyes looked briefly into mine, then glanced away, but in that moment I was sure she loved me in return.

I lifted Rose to her feet, and we went to settle ourselves by the fire, to talk of all that had happened since last we met. They wept despairingly as they spoke of

63

their mother's fatal accident, and it was then I noticed how strained and ill both young women were. They had been through a great deal, and it had aged them. I was overwhelmed with pity, and ready with a few conventional words of condolence, but I felt singularly helpless to give any real comfort. Presently, their weeping ceased.

Rose looked up with a watery smile and said "But we are not alone any more, Barbara. We have Myles, and our sorrow will pass."

Barbara was frowning. "Yes, it will pass" she said sadly. "But it will take time for, although she was not my real mother, I loved her just as deeply as if she were." Then, turning to me, her eyes astute and unblinking, she asked why I had not written for such a long time. "It was not kind", she said quietly. "Your silence led us to take for granted the news that you had been killed."

I hesitated for a moment, remembering that after all was said and done William was their brother, and I did not want to add to their troubles by denouncing him. But, in the end, I decided to be frank for it would come out eventually when I took my case to court. "It will make hard hearing" I said, then, speaking sternly and without ease, I unfolded the whole sorry story. Their eyes did not leave my face as I spoke of the contempt I felt for William. At the same time, I felt their sympathy was with me, and that they believed I had been greatly wronged. Nevertheless, when I let fall that I had it in mind to contest my grandfather's will and so bring William's treachery out into the open, their faces flushed with embarrassment. They stared at me apprehensively, and there was a long silence.

Then Barbara came and laid a hand on my arm. "Please leave things as they are" she pleaded, her expression full of pain. "I feel sure you will gain nothing if you go to law, and there will be a lot of unnecessary and hurtful scandal."

"All the same it will be worth a try" I said. "William should not be allowed to get off scot free with my inheritance." I heard Rose gasp, then she started to sob uncontrollably, and I began to feel frustrated and uncertain. Bitter hatred and resentment against their brother nagged at me, but I could not add to their trials after all they had suffered, so in the end, hiding my sense of outrage, I agreed to let the matter drop for, as Barbara had already pointed out, there was only a slim chance I would be successful. In some strange way, as soon as I made this decision, I felt exhilarated. I welcomed the challenge to make something of myself without the benefit of inherited riches and, besides, the two young women smiled at each other with such evident relief that it seemed worth the yielding just to witness their happiness.

That night after dinner, when we had all calmed down somewhat, we talked easily together, and I was able to enquire more deeply into their affairs. They disclosed that William had agreed to let them live at Ellanbane for as long as they wished, and had settled an adequate income on them which would cease if and when they married. "Thomas Cleator", said Barbara, "has been left in full charge here as before" – then added, in almost a whisper, "Thomas and I are to be married early next year". I gazed at her aghast. This was the bitterest news of my whole life and I did not know how to bear it for, ever since we bade one another goodbye as I left to join the army, I had been resolved to marry her. Somehow there was this understanding between us without anything having been said, except through various kind messages conveyed to one another in my grandfather's correspondence.

I was now almost thirty years of age, and had never before known such overwhelming love for a woman. All evening I had been turning things over in my mind, and had decided to ask her to marry me as soon as possible for, although I was no longer heir to a vast estate, I could prevail on the Derby family to find me some work to do here in the Isle of Man, and in this way we could still be near to Rose. But now this plan was doomed before it had a chance of success. Murmuring bleakly that I hoped Thomas and she would be happy, I was enough in command of myself to talk of other things.

First of all, I wanted to know how George Quayle and Kitty were faring. They were well, Barbara told me, and young Huan had grown into a fine young man. "But Kitty took the news of your death very badly" she added. "For a time she was quite ill, and George was worried about her." I felt a great lifting of the spirits to know that Kitty still cared for me, although I was sorry to have caused her this pain. I heard too with sadness that my little dog, Scamp, had died, which was of course only to be expected after all these years, but Peggy was still alive and well, but too old for any riding. Then, in turn, I entertained them with the strange tale of my meeting with Jacques, and showed them the Mylecraine Cross, which they thought very beautiful, as indeed it was. After a while, Rose announced she was going to bed. She was tired after all the excitement of the day.

As soon as the door closed behind her, I went over and stood beside Barbara. I told her I loved her, that I was totally obsessed by her and I begged her to break off her engagement to Thomas Cleator and marry me. She turned her face away as I spoke, but suddenly, without a word, she rose, put her arms around my neck and kissed me with a singular urgency. Then she let go and, leaning against me, began to weep.

"I love you, darling Myles, so very much, but you have left it too late" she sobbed. "I waited for you for a long time, for I knew you would ask me to marry you when you returned, but when the news came that you had been killed, I agreed to marry Thomas. I wanted a home and children before I was too old, and Thomas is of the same mind."

"But do you love him?" I asked, my heart full of jealousy.

"No", she said, "I do not love him in the way I love you, but I am fond of him and respect him. He is a good man, and loves me deeply, and I will not hurt him by going back on my word."

I tried hard to make her change her mind but she was adamant. Heartstricken, and miserable, I went off to bed, cursing my luck and blaming myself, as I had done so many times recently, for ever having left Ellanbane in the first place.

CHAPTER SIXTEEN

When I awoke next morning, I was amazed that I had slept well and so escaped from misery in spite of my bitter disappointment. I lay for a while and let other more pleasant thoughts float through my mind, and began to plan my life afresh. For a start, I would forget Barbara and ask Rose to marry me, confident in the hope that she would have me. She was a dear girl and I loved her – not in the passionate way I had loved Barbara but in a more gentle, protective fashion. Then I would return to Leyden and the army, taking her with me for, if there were any more wars to be fought even in some far off country, I could safely leave her for a while with my Separatist friends there. The prospect pleased me, and I felt happy and anxiety-free for the first time in many months.

It was early, but I rose and breakfasted alone, then went to seek out Peggy, my little mare. I found her in a shed at the far end of the paddock behind the house and, as soon as I opened the wide wooden door and called her, she ambled slowly towards me and nuzzled her head against my chest. She had been well cared for, and was sleek and round as an apple. I was overjoyed that she had not forgotten me, and stood for a long time stroking her muzzle, patting her and talking to her softly.

I had been there for nearly an hour when Rose appeared at the door, cheerfully calling my name. I went forward and took her hand in mine. She had come to tell me that she had just been over to Glentrammon to break the news to George and Kitty that I was here at Ellanbane, alive and well. "You had better go along there soon as Kitty is wild with delight, and they are both longing to see you."

I could feel her fingers in mine and I gave them a gentle squeeze. Then, turning to her, I took her in my arms and kissed her. "I want you to marry me, Rose," I whispered. She looked at me, brilliant eyed and blushing.

"Oh Myles, how wonderful! When shall it be?"

"As soon as possible" I said and kissed her again, but, as I held her pressed close to me, I imagined she was Barbara, and I was ashamed. We stood there with my arm around her, her head nestled on my shoulder, and made plans for the future, oblivious of Peggy, who whinnied once or twice, then went back to eating from a rack of hay in a corner.

Time seemed to fly, and it was mid-morning before I left for Glentrammon. I asked Rose to come with me, but she wanted to go back to the house to tell Barbara her news. "She will be so pleased for us to be married" she said, and I

66

had a little vicarious pleasure in hoping that Barbara would be sorry for having turned me down in favour of Thomas Cleator.

Kitty and George were leaning on the farm gate watching for me and, as I rounded the corner of the lane, Kitty, with a whoop of joy, picked up her skirts and came, running, to put her arms around me. She held me closely for a long time and I began to think she would never let me go. Happy tears were rolling down her cheeks. "Oh thank God!" she kept saying over and over again. George was less exuberant, but in his own way he showed plainly enough that he was pleased to see me. He kept pumping my hand up and down, his face alive with pleasure. He was "off to the mart" this morning to buy some in-calf cows, but would be back within the hour to hear all my news. So Kitty and I walked together towards the house, her arm tucked in mine and, once inside, we sat down comfortably beside the fire, in the pleasant farm kitchen, and talked, delighted to be in one another's company again.

Affairs had gone very well at Glentrammon, Kitty informed me. The land was in good heart and the stock thriving. Then, since Caesar Mylecraine, Betsey, his sister, and also his daughter Voirrey, had died, all his money and land had come to George as next of kin. So now they were quite rich and had bought a large farm at Sulby, and they would be moving there at Hollantide. When I asked her about Huan their son, her eyes kindled and a tender smile spread across her face. It was patently obvious that she adored him. "He is cleaning out the cow houses this morning" she said, "but he will be in soon. He has heard such a lot about you, and feels he knows you already from the letters you sent us through your grandfather when you were in Ostend. He is a fine boy, Myles." She had spoken lovingly and full of pride. She wanted me to love him too.

Not long after he came walking in, and gave me a tremendous shock. He was a tall young fellow, slim, handsome, broad of shoulder, narrow hipped and the living image of Jacques the Frenchman in his prime. The same bold black eyes and roguish smile, the same swashbuckling gait and jaunty manner. Nevertheless, he was pleasant and friendly, and I liked him. He stayed talking for a while with just the right amount of shy deference to please his elders, then, with a cheerful smile, went off to feed some pigs.

As the door closed behind him, I gazed at Kitty, completely at a loss for words. She was looking down, nervously clasping and unclasping her hands, and for a while there was utter silence between us. Then she said gently "So you see the likeness, Myles?"

"Indeed I do" I said. "They are alike as two peas."

She raised her head, and looked at me directly. "It is not what you think my dear, for Huan is not my child." Then, looking a little past my face as if into the distance, she told me a poignant story.

"If you remember," she began, "I nearly died in childbirth, and have been unable to have another baby?" I nodded hesitantly. It was a long time ago and I was so young that I had almost forgotten. "Well," Kitty went on, "a few hours after he was born, our little son died. Betsey Mylecraine, who attended me at the

67

birth, took him away while I was hardly conscious, and too ill to know what had happened. She put her niece, Voirrey's baby, in his place and buried our child just inside the churchyard wall." Here Kitty looked straight at me, her expression full of sorrow. "It grieves me", she said, "that I do not know the exact spot." We both sat silent for a while. I was leaning forward, waiting for her to continue, and feeling desperately sorry for her.

At last she said: "I never guessed there was anything wrong with Voirrey. I had not seen her about for some time, but supposed she was busy preparing for her wedding to her young sheep farmer. But apparently when he discovered she was pregnant, he abandoned all plans for the marriage. However, Voirrey was well able to keep her secret. Her father was dead, her Aunt Betsey was attending her as well as me and our babies were born within days of each other, which made the exchange easy. For many years, I truly believed Huan to be our son, but I could never understand why he looked so like Jacques."

"And what did George say?" I burst out. "He must have noticed the likeness too."

"Oh yes, he did," said Kitty, "and one day he asked me if there had been anything serious between Jacques and me. He said that, even if there had, I was not to worry, it would make no difference to his love for me, but he wanted the truth. And do you know, Myles," she said, her face transfigured with joy, "he believed me when I told him that I was as puzzled as he was, and that I had never deceived him or been unfaithful to him at any time in my life."

"When did you discover the truth about the boy?" I asked.

"Only a year ago when Voirrey died. She left a letter to be forwarded to me after her death, explaining all. It was lucky George was out when I opened it, for he believes Huan to be his son, and it would break his heart if he found he was not, for he dotes on the boy. It has been a relief to tell you all this" she said, gazing at me intently, "and I know you will tell no one else."

"Of course", I said, "the story is safe with me." Stirred by a surge of love for her, I put my arms around her and kissed her, and suddenly she was on the edge of tears.

A little while later George and Huan came in for their midday meal. Kitty insisted that I joined them, and it was like old times, sitting together around the white scrubbed table to enjoy Kitty's tasty cooking. There was great excitement when, before we started the meal, I drew the silver Cross from my pocket and handed it to George with a shortened explanation of how it had been acquired, for now it was rightfully his. George thanked me, and passed it to Huan and Kitty to examine. Huan's eyes sparkled with inquisitiveness. "Where did it come from, Father?" he asked. But George said he would tell them the whole story some other time. First he wanted to hear all my news.

They listened spellbound as, during the meal, I told them of how I had been robbed of my inheritance, and their eyes were fully of anger and pity. However, I assured them I had come to terms with this change in my prospects, and was now full of zest for the future. Then, when I let fall that Rose and I were soon to be

68

married, there was an outcry of congratulations, but Kitty gave me a searching glance. "I always believed it would be Barbara" she said, "but, of course, that would have been impossible now that she is promised to Thomas Cleator." I did not reply to this, but I had a strong suspicion that Kitty guessed the whole truth of the matter.

It was late afternoon when I left for Ellanbane. George came with me to the gate and I could see he was nerving himself to tell me something. He threw an arm across my shoulders, half-turned towards me and looked into my eyes. "Did you notice how like Huan is to Jacques?" he asked. He was speaking in an agitated whisper.

"Well," I said, hardly knowing how to reply and hedging a little, "He is very dark, of course."

"Jacques is Huan's father" George burst out. "But I love him as much as if he were mine. Betsey Mylecraine sent for me when she was dying, and told me he was really her niece Voirrey's child and that she had put him in our dead baby's place a few hours after his birth. Kitty has no doubt he is our son, and it would break her heart if she were to find out he was not, so please keep it to yourself. I am telling you all this for her sake, so that you would not misjudge her."

"I will disclose it to no one, George," I said as we shook hands in parting, and I went off deeply moved at the great love these two dear friends of mine had for one another.

CHAPTER SEVENTEEN

On the 23rd of December, Rose and I were married at Lezayre Church with only Barbara, Thomas Cleator, George Quayle and Kitty present at the wedding. Owing to family mourning, we wanted it to be private.

Then one morning, shortly after Christmas, which was also spent very quietly, we rode across to Castletown to visit the Karrans, for I wanted to show off my pretty young bride. Joe and Edward were without doubt pleased to see us both, but all their attention was fixed upon Rose, who responded at once to their friendly welcome. She had the special gift of liking almost everyone she met, and the Karrans were no exception. In all her well regulated protected life, she had never before been a guest in a fisherman's cottage, but she was unreservedly interested in everything they did, particularly in their method of catching fish, and how they disposed of their catch. All her questions were easy and straightforward, and I could see they were taken with her, especially when Edward turned to me thoughtfully and said "Rose will be all you could possibly wish for in a partner, and I think you are a very lucky fellow, Myles." I glanced across at Rose, who was blushing with pleasure at Edward's remark. Putting an arm around her waist, I drew her close and smiled at her with special affection. "I am sure you are right, Edward," I said, "for that is also my opinion."

After sharing a meal with them, I thought it well to pay a duty call on Lady Derby and her son, Lord Strange, at Castle Rushen. "It is only polite to let them know we are married" I said to Rose. My grandfather would have wished it, for the Derby family were his valued friends as well as kinsfolk.

We stayed only a short time at the Castle for we wanted to be back at Ellanbane before nightfall but, as it turned out, it was fortunate for us that we had gone there for when, in the course of conversation, we let fall that we would soon be leaving for Holland, Lord Strange said he would be going to London himself in three days and invited us to travel with him thus far. He would, he told us, be sailing from Derbyhaven for Liverpool on a Derby ship, and thence by private coach to London. I was more than pleased to comply for it would make the journey so much more comfortable for Rose.

Consequently, soon after daybreak on the appointed day, we set off in the carriage from Ellanbane. Thomas Cleator was driving us and, to my surprise, he seemed to accept without question his role of superior manservant, yet at the same time retaining his self-respect and dignity. Also there was a certain attraction in

70

his dark, good looks, and I began to understand what Barbara saw in him.

This time there was no sadness when we left, for I felt quite sure I would be able to arrange for frequent leaves of absence, since there seemed little likelihood of any more wars in Europe. So I made it quite clear we would be back again soon, little knowing that neither Rose nor, probably, I would ever again set foot on our beloved Island. As we drove off, I turned to wave goodbye to Barbara who was standing at the open door to bid us farewell. She was gazing straight at me, her eyes sharp with pain, and in that moment I knew that I would always care for her deeply, even though I loved little Rose with all my heart.

Throughout our long drive to Derbyhaven, Rose talked eagerly of how much she was looking forward to our new life together. She gave out happiness, and was as full of excitement and joy as a little girl. The day turned out to be sunny and unusually mild for early January, one of winter's pet days, and, as we cast off from the little breakwater at Derbyhaven, the winds, too, proved favourable. Accordingly, the compact little ship made good time and we arrived at the port of Liverpool in mid-afternoon. A splendidly equipped coach was waiting for us there, and we travelled to London in fine style, staying comfortably each night at the great houses of friends of the Derby family.

Lord Strange was a pleasant enough travelling companion, but I found him singularly humourless, and he talked continuously about himself in a tired monotonous voice. Rose, however, listened to him with gentle attention, and he seemed captivated with her. He was a tall, well-favoured young man, and I must confess to feeling a little jealous of his obvious good looks, and also somewhat put out by his over-fond attitude towards Rose. So, on the whole, I was glad to part company with him when we arrived at London, yet at the same time grateful to him for making our journey so easy.

Within hours of arriving in the capital, we found a ship bound for Holland. Three days later we reached Leyden. I had written to John Robinson before Christmas, informing him of our forthcoming marriage, also of the approximate date of our arrival, and when at last we knocked on the door of Groenepoort, it was quickly thrown open and John Robinson ushered us into the main meeting hall to be welcomed warmly by the rest of the Robinson family, as well as several of the members of the Church, who had been meeting together in "oversight".

Then, a little to my dismay, John took his place by my side and, with a hand on my shoulder, said a long prayer of thanksgiving for our safe arrival. This was punctuated by a loud chorus of "Amens" and "Hallelujahs" from the rest of the company. Rose, not at all nonplussed, treated these new acquaintances as if she had known them all her life. "They are good people", she said to me later, "and I know I shall be happy amongst them."

The Robinsons kindly invited us to stay with them until we found somewhere to live, and within days we had rented a furnished house on the Rapensburg Quay — a pretty house with stepped and curved gables of classic Dutch design, bright and airy and with a splendid view across the placid waters of the canal. We settled down there extremely happily. I returned to my military employment and Rose

71

was much occupied with her housewifely duties, cleaning and poluhing, until everywhere in the house shone, and shopping frequently in Leyden's picturesque little market lanes. Also she entered into all the Separatist wives' activities, attending the "Women's Meetings", "Sewing Classes", "Children's Services" and even an occasional prayer meeting. On Sundays she was usually present at Groenepoort morning meeting and, although she had all her life been a practising member of the Church of England, she took this strange, wordy and over-exuberant form of worship in her stride. Nevertheless, she often admitted to me that she longed for the more peaceful and dignified services of her own Church, and in this she never altered.

I, however, did not go again to any of the meetings, yet still remained friendly with John Robinson and many of the congregation. We were pleased to have made such good friends, and there was much visiting between our houses.

We had been settled in Leyden, blissfully content with our lot, for close on ten years when one evening, as we were sitting before a comfortable fire with candles lit and curtains drawn, enjoying a game of chess, there came a knock on the door. I opened it to John Robinson. "I am sorry to disturb you, Myles," he said, "but I have a proposition to put to you both."

He came and sat with us beside the fire. He seemed strangely excited, yet at the same time sober and tight-lipped. We spoke generalities for a while, about the severe weather and the high cost of living here in Leyden, when suddenly he leaned forward, both hands on his knees, and began to speak earnestly. "See here," he began, "this is what I have come to tell you. Our congregation have decided to emigrate to America for the purpose of establishing a colony there, and arrangements to this end have been in progress for some time, although up to date the setbacks have been enormous."

"But why, John?" I exclaimed. "Surely you are well enough settled here and enjoy the utmost religious freedom amongst the Dutch people."

"There is a good deal more to it than that", he replied, "and I am afraid it has become quite necessary for us to leave." He began to explain their reasons carefully. "You see, my friends," he said, "for some time now our elders have become increasingly worried by the poverty in which most of our people find themselves here. Many are feeling old age approaching, and have been compelled to send their children out to work in order to keep themselves alive. These children have been forced to work so hard that their bodies have become bowed under the strain, and they are growing old before their time, physically weakened in the prime of their young lives. A more immediate danger is the temptation the children themselves face through living among the pleasure-loving Dutch. Some are sliding into extravagant ways, defying their parents, and many are leaving home to live sinful and worldly lives far away from parental supervision. Added to all this, we are gaining no converts. The Dutch are satisfied with their own Church and have no 'conviction of sin'. YET GOD'S WORK MUST GO ON." Here he crashed his fist down on our chess table, making the pieces rattle and jump all over the place.

72

Rose and I sat in silence, too surprised to say anything as John continued to talk. "Naturally," he said, "having heard good reports of the adventures of Sir Walter Raleigh and others, we have made numerous enquiries about land in the Far West of America and have discovered that the chief perils to face there would be from hordes of savage Indians who would not hesitate to attack white men, then scalp and torture them. As you well know, we Separatists are not a fighting people, and are therefore unskilled in the art of war. So we have been meeting together at Groenepoort to talk over the Indian problem, what to do about it, and to pray for God's guidance. Some of our members believe we should simply trust in God to protect us: more down to earth brethren think it wise to be well supplied with firearms. But others contend that, if one of our objects in going to America is to bring Christianity to the Indians, then we must not carry a Bible in one hand and a harquebus in the other."

Here John paused, and looked at us both across the fireplace with a worried expression. "I have suggested, Myles," he said, "that you be invited to join our company as military adviser and leader, and, after some controversy, it has been agreed that I sound out your feelings on the matter. Will you come with us?"

I had known, as soon as he began to tell his long tale, that this was coming, and I must admit that the adventurous character of the project appealed to me. The spice of danger, the idea of life in a new country, the vast possibilities of colonisation in America, excited me. Yet I could not give him the answer he was looking for right away. "I must", I said, "first of all discuss the whole matter and its implications with Rose."

"I understand", said John, "but I would like your answer as quickly as possible."

After he left, Rose and I talked over the whole affair and, to my great joy, Rose agreed it would be a most wonderful experience, adding that she was willing and happy to go with me anywhere in the wide world I wished to venture. I thought it only fair to remind her that probably we would not be able to visit the Island again for some years to come, but even that prospect did not deter her, and I began to realise she was as eager for the adventure as I was.

Next day I went over to Groenepoort and told John Robinson that Rose and I were ready to go with them. "How splendid" he said. Then, laying a hand on my shoulder, he paused for a moment and looked straight at me and continued: "I wish you could find it in your heart to join our congregation in Christian fellowship."

I shook my head. "No, John," I replied, "that is the only reservation I make, that membership of the Church is not to be a condition for the post."

"So be it, Myles," he said with a rueful smile, "but I tell you, my friend, that I believe you live more of a Christian life than many Christians I know, and I have always found you to be thoroughly dependable and trustworthy. I am sure you will be a tower of strength to the whole company, for we will all be pilgrims in a strange land when we reach America."

CHAPTER EIGHTEEN

Preparations for the departure of the Separatists soon got under way in spite of many problems. These, I might add, were mostly of their own making for, although they were an immensely honourable and courageous group of people, they were also extremely contentious. They argued, and wrangled, continually about whether it was best to go to Guiana or Virginia. Furthermore, they were unhappy about some of the conditions in the contract drawn up by the merchant company which was to sponsor the venture. In the end, many withdrew from the enterprise altogether, and this posed a major problem for the company. They had risked their money solely in the hope of rich returns in the shape of profitable cargoes from the new colony. Therefore reinforcements had to be found if the emigrants were to be strong enough to survive the difficulties facing them in the desolate land across the Atlantic Ocean. So they signed up extra colonists in London, recruiting them with no regard at all for their religious beliefs. It was no concern of theirs, they said, how they prayed as long as they were willing workers and made a profit for the company. These observations filled me with misgivings. I could see a tricky situation arising, seeing that the Separatists were in the main confirmed bigots. They cherished an unshaken belief that anyone outside their Faith was bound for hell fire. Moreover, they proclaimed these beliefs to all they met, in the hope of saving souls from damnation, and I was afraid this mixed company would make awkward bedfellows.

However, in spite of doubts and uncertainties, arrangements went slowly forward. The whole congregation put their money into a common fund, which was to be drawn on when necessary. They bought a ship, the *Speedwell*, a vessel of about 60 tons, which arrived from England to take the emigrants to Southampton. There they were to be joined by other Separatists wishing to accompany them to America. Unfortunately, the vessel proved to be in a bad condition. She had to be refitted at great expense, and was obliged to lie to at Delft Haven where new and larger masts were stepped in and a fresh suit of sails purchased for her.

In the meantime, I resigned from the army and, while waiting for the ship to be put in repair, spent much of my time in the University library. I wanted to find out all I could about America, but the knowledge I obtained was meagre. I found that, although many adventurers and explorers had landed there after its discovery by Columbus in 1492, very little had been written on the subject.

Many years had elapsed since John Cabot had sailed from Bristol with the

74

main object of finding a sea route to India and had inadvertently discovered Newfoundland. Yet it was still an unknown continent, even though more recently Raleigh, Gilbert, Drake and Grenville had all landed on its shores. Grenville had founded a settlement in Virginia which unhappily ended in failure, and it was not until 1606 that the Virginia Company was formed. In the following year the first English settlement was established, under the leadership of Captain John Smith, on the banks of the James River. The French founded Quebec in 1608 and the Dutch, three years later, started a settlement on the Hudson River. Then, not long ago, Captain John Smith had successfully petitioned Charles, Prince of Wales, to name part of Virginia "New England", and it was at some point on this coast that the Separatists decided to make for.

This then was the disappointingly small amount of information I was able to pick up at the library. I had wanted above all to discover the habits of the Indian tribes with whom we would have to deal, their language and method of warfare. Nevertheless, I had gathered some knowledge of the geographical features of the country, which was in the end to prove most useful. Eventually the *Speedwell* was ready to leave. The great day of departure arrived and the "Pilgrim Fathers", as they now called themselves, proclaimed a day of solemn humiliation. They always did this on momentous occasions, when much time was spent in praying and weeping.

I did not attend, but stayed at home to settle our affairs before leaving and to write to George and Kitty, and to Barbara, telling them of our latest plans, and that it would be some considerable time before we would be able to visit the Island. Rose, however, went to the service and heard John Robinson preach a sermon that took nearly all day. After that there was a feast at Groenepoort in honour of those about to depart. All tears were dried, and the whole company enjoyed the banquet immensely, eating and drinking to their hearts content. The feasting was interspersed freely with Christian discourse and much psalm singing and prayers. Soon after, at sunrise on the 21st of July 1620, we set out by canal for Delft Haven about twenty miles to the south. Most of the friends at Groenepoort travelled with us and others came from as far as Amsterdam to see us off. Many were remaining behind only for a short time and proposed to follow on when the first contingent had established themselves.

Therefore it was decided that Pastor Robinson should stay behind at Groenepoort and accompany them when the time was right, while Ruling Elder Brewster went with the emigrants. On arriving at Delft Haven, there was yet another feast with more Scriptural discourse and expressions of Christian love. That night was spent ashore, and early next morning we boarded the *Speedwell*. All the friends that had accompanied us came on board to exchange last farewells and, when it was time to set sail, John Robinson fell to his knees on the quayside, and those that were staying knelt with him as he gave his blessing. With tears running down his cheeks, he commended us all to the Lord. And so the first company of "Pilgrims" left the place which had been their home for almost twelve years.

The full complement sailing together in the *Speedwell* numbered just under fifty souls, almost half of them children. William Bradford, an elder of the Church, and his wife, Dorothy, had decided to leave their son, John, a little boy of only five years, in the care of the Robinsons. Alas, the poor little fellow never saw his mother again, nor his father for seven years. His heartbreaking appeals and frightened cries at parting tore my heart asunder, and Rose was appalled. "I cannot understand", she said, her eyes full of unshed tears, "how the Bradfords can inflict this suffering on their little boy, how they can stand seeing him so distressed." I agreed with her, and firmly believe this very sad parting to be the cause of Dorothy Bradford's sudden death some months later. Many believed she committed suicide, but this was never spoken of, as it was regarded a heinous offence against the laws of God to take one's own life.

CHAPTER NINETEEN

So the *Speedwell* got slowly under way, with the English ensign fluttering gaily at her mastheads. Everyone, Rose and I included, crowded the decks to wave a last farewell to those left behind. As I stood there with my arm about her shoulders, I wondered if we would ever see any of them again, and I felt a twinge of anxiety. The enormity of the adventure suddenly began to dawn on me. America was immensely far away, and the intervening ocean so perilous and unpredictable, that I was beginning to wish I had not subjected Rose to such danger. As if reading my thoughts, she turned and smiled at me affectionately. "Do you know, Myles," she said, "I feel this is the beginning of a wonderful adventure." She was looking at me without a trace of fear, so confident that all would be well, that my qualms seemed groundless.

A salvo of cannon boomed a parting salute as the ship moved into the Maas channel. With a fair wind behind her, she quickly gathered speed and we were soon past the Hook of Holland and out into the wider waters of the North Sea. Here we met problems, for the *Speedwell* turned out to be a rickety vessel. She lurched badly and shipped masses of water even under easy sail. This caused the skipper great anxiety, besides giving us all several severe wettings. Nevertheless, we continued to make good time and three days later arrived at Southampton. We dropped anchor at the West Quay alongside another ship, the *Mayflower*, a fine vessel almost three times larger than the *Speedwell*. She had been waiting for us there for several days, having arrived from London with the emigrants recruited by the merchant company. These strangers greeted us enthusiastically, and there were mutual expressions of friendship amongst us, with much to-ing and fro-ing between the two ships.

Next day, as it was soon to be her birthday, I took Rose into Southampton to buy her a present. It was a pleasant enough little town, but very neglected with its walls urgently in need of repair, crumbling pavements not fit to walk upon and filthy streets. However, we managed to find one or two reasonably clean thoroughfares with bright well-stocked shops, and Rose was delighted when I bought her a pretty blue enamel locket set with seed pearls. I also purchased a parcel of books on divers subjects, which I hoped would make good reading for us both on the long journey ahead.

We had expected to set sail almost immediately, but several days passed with no definite headway made towards departure, so I sought out Elder Bradford and asked him why we were being delayed. "There is nothing to be gained and a lot to lose by waiting here", I told him, "for soon the weather will be against us." To my disgust, he disclosed that affairs were in a frightful muddle.

The Pilgrims had been unable to gather together enough money for all their needs, owing to the cost already sustained of repairs to the *Speedwell*. In addition, the faults which had come to light on the journey from Holland would also need correcting. Furthermore, a dispute had arisen with the sponsoring company over amended articles in the agreement between themselves and the Pilgrims. These differed greatly from those agreed upon at Leyden, for they would reduce the Pilgrims almost to the status of slaves, oblige them to work almost every day to fill the pockets of the company and leave them scarcely any opportunity to build up a prosperous colony for themselves. This new contract the Pilgrims resolutely refused to sign, and in retaliation the company declined, point blank, to supply any more money and left us all high and dry at the last moment. They saddled us with liabilities of £100 which had to be paid before the two vessels left port, and this came as a great shock, for each day we stayed in port made our journey into violent inclement weather ever more probable.

To my mind, the only possible way out of the difficulty was to sell some of our provisions to the value of the sum needed. Such a step would, of course, mean short commons, perhaps even semi-starvation for all of us, but after some deliberation and discussions with the leaders, it was reluctantly decided to do as I suggested. Then, free from this burden of debt, we bent all our energies to the final arrangements for departure.

I saw to it that sufficient powder and arms were shipped to meet all contingencies. Helmets, coats of mail and swords were also included in the cause of self-defence, which was to be my special province. Eventually, on the 15th of August 1620, the two ships set off. But the start was a bad one. Contrary winds caused a great loss of time and, worse still, the Captain of the *Speedwell* suddenly announced that the ship was leaking badly. There was nothing for it but to run into Dartmouth for repairs. After some delay we set off again, but in no time at all this unstable vessel sprang an even more serious leak. Both ships turned back to Plymouth and it was decided to dispense altogether with the *Speedwell* and send her back to London. Most of her passengers transferred to the *Mayflower*, but twenty Pilgrims turned back. They decided to quit after having suffered dreadfully from seasickness. Even so, the *Mayflower* was now packed to the gunwales with 102 passengers besides the officers and crew.

Little more than a third of these passengers were from Leyden: forty-one to be precise – seventeen men, ten women and fourteen children. The greater number was composed of "Strangers" from London and south-eastern England, and these were mostly orthodox Anglicans. The first leg of the journey went very well, even in such cramped quarters, and everyone seemed determined to make the best of things. The *Mayflower* was a fine ship, above average in size, and with a good following wind we were in mid-Atlantic and still forging steadily ahead by the end of September. Unfortunately, boredom now began to set in on the overcrowded

78

ship. As I had foreseen, quarrels arose. The Strangers could not put up with the pious language of the Pilgrims and were affronted by their continual efforts to make converts of them. The sailors also hated the devout Pilgrims and went out of their way to shock and torment them with vile oaths and obscene talk. When the Pilgrims admonished them, no matter how meekly, they would "curse and swear most bitterly". Their ringleader, a great blustering oafish fellow, continually derided and taunted the many poor souls lying about helpless in the throes of seasickness.

He constantly told them how much he was looking forward to burying them all at sea "and then make merry with what they left behind". This terrified the poor sufferers out of their wits, and one morning, when I was told he had reduced many of the women to tears, I could stand it no longer. I leapt up the companionway to the upper deck where he and his messmates were shortening sail in anticipation of the equinoxial gales we were certain to encounter.

They all stopped work, and were gazing at me silently with impudent stares as I crossed the deck. I stood facing the bully. "What the devil do you mean by terrifying those poor sick women below?" I yelled at the top of my voice.

He immediately let go of the rope he was holding and made a menacing gesture with his forearm. "Be off, you little bastard", he cried, "or I will knock you to kingdom come!" Then, with a volley of oaths spewing from his lips, he turned to his cronies with an evil leer. "Take a look at the Pilgrims' captain" he said: "they will have nothing to fear while they have Captain Shrimp to protect them!" There were loud guffaws and shouts of laughter from all sides.

At this my temper, which has always been hard to control, got the upper hand. I rushed towards him with lowered head, and butted him hard in the stomach. To my surprise and great delight this winded him. His breath came out in a loud grunt, and he bent almost double. Seeing his great ugly face nearly on a level with my shoulder, I dealt him a swift uppercut with all the force I could muster.

He turned a half somersault and hit his head with a mighty thud against the ship's rail. I stood for a moment, gazing at him with supreme contempt, as he tried to rise but could not. He lay there white-faced and dazed, unable to comprehend what had happened to him. His companions gaped at him open-mouthed and bewildered. Then one of them went over with a pocket flask and poured some spirits down his throat. Seconds later he opened his eyes, shook his head from side to side vehemently as if to clear it, then shot me a look of intense hatred, mingled with fear, and I could not resist shaking my fist at him and cursing him loud and long. Before returning below, I assured the whole bunch of them that, if ever again I heard any one of them refer to me as Captain Shrimp, I would do the same for him.

Next morning the fellow complained of a great sickness. By afternoon he was dead, and his body was the first to go overboard. His death had a most salutary effect on both the crew and the quarrelling passengers, for they were all quite sure it was the hand of the Lord upon him. However, I believe that my set-to with him also had something to do with it, albeit unintentionally.

Meantime the weather suddenly changed. Violent storms arose of such fury that the helmsmen found it extremely difficult to hold the ship into the wind as she plunged into wild mountainous seas. She pitched and rolled so violently that she sprang leaks in the decks and superstructure, which sent cascades of icy water down upon us as we lay in our bunks. We could not keep warm, and sleep was well nigh impossible owing to the roaring of the wind in the rigging, and the continual noise of heavy seas battering the ship's sides. The air in our sleeping quarters now became disgustingly foul, full of the stench of vomited, undigested food, and one of the Pilgrims, John Howland, could stand it no longer. He went on deck for a breath of fresh air, and was immediately swept overboard. Luckily for him he was able to hang on to some trailing topsail halyards and, although at one time he was several fathoms under water, he was eventually pulled in with a boathook.

The fierce storm gave no sign of abating: in fact it grew ever worse, and the constant buffeting of the gales caused a main beam amidships to crack under the strain. It caved in with a loud report, and we all thought we were done for, but by great good chance one of the Pilgrims had brought with him a large iron screw, presumably part of a printing press. I never did discover why he brought it, but it turned out to be a great blessing, for we used it to raise the beam and force it into place. Then the ship's carpenter reinforced it and secured it with a timber braced against the main deck.

Altogether it was a dreadful journey full of discomfort. We suffered miserably from the freezing cold, most of us wet through daily, and all of us short of food. I was profoundly troubled as to how Rose would stand up to such hardship, but I need not have worried. She soon found her sea-legs and was able to negotiate the heaving decks almost as well as the sailors. She kept a weather eye on the children to see they did not fall over the side and kept them amused by telling stories and playing games with them. I was constantly amazed at her courage and resourcefulness, and was immensely proud of her. At the very height of the storm, Elizabeth Hopkins, one of the Pilgrims, gave birth to a baby boy, a bonny child whom they aptly named Oceanus. Then, sadly, on the 6th of November, a young man, William Butten, died, and his remains were committed reverently to the deep the next day. It says much for the stamina of the rest of us that we all survived the terrible conditions.

At last, after long beating about at sea, the look-out caught a glimpse of a faint blur off the starboard bow, and the cry of "Land-Ahoy", so long awaited and almost despaired of, brought us all running to catch our first glimpse of America. We gazed at the faint dark coast line with unfeigned thankfulness, full of joy that the end of the nightmarish journey was in sight. But our troubles were not yet over. The skipper announced that this land was Cape Cod, discovered in 1602 by Bartholemew Gosnold, and had received its name from the abundance of codfish in the harbour. This was considerably to the northward of the place the Pilgrims had intended to land. Nevertheless, for reasons of his own, he had brought us here instead of to the neighbourhood of the Hudson river.

Later we discovered that he was anxious to sail back to England as soon as possible, but now he was instructed to tack about for the south. Unfortunately, the ship ran into a network of dangerous shoals and breakers, and it was decided to return to Cape Cod. The helm was put hard over, and we headed back up the coast to lie all night with only a gentle breeze blowing.

In the morning, we rounded the Cape and, as the anchor went down and the decks underfoot became steady, a thrill of joy went through us all, and everyone was looking forward to going ashore. But first some serious business had to be undertaken. Before landing, all adult males had to sign a contract in which they agreed to submit to all laws and ordinances that might be framed by the leaders. This was done because some of the Strangers had become defiant, declaring they were at liberty to go anywhere they wished and to work entirely for themselves. They wanted nothing to do with the sponsoring company to which we still owed a considerable sum, and to whom we were still bound by the Leyden Contract. They maintained that they had agreed to go to Virginia, and not New England, and that this made the patent they held null and void. However, one of the Company, John Carver, was elected Governor for a year and he was a strong determined man who firmly put down the mutinous Strangers.

Then it was proposed that I go ashore in the long-boat with a dozen well-armed men to reconnoitre and also to bring back much needed supplies of wood and water. As we got under way, Rose was leaning over the ship's side with some of the other wives to see us set sail. I waved to her and, standing with one hand shading her eyes, she waved back. This was the first time we had been parted since our marriage, and I was moved with a great rush of love for her. I could not be sure, for there was some distance between us, but I thought her expression was both dejected and apprehensive, and I could not help wishing that I did not have to leave her. For all that, it was good to step ashore and walk upright and normally again.

We were now in a singularly empty country but, through the hazy November daylight, a thickly wooded hinterland loomed ominously ahead. This, I thought, might prove to be a splendid cover for both wild men and wild beasts, and, on the alert myself, I warned the others also to keep a sharp lookout. But that day we saw no human creature, nor alas any water either. The woods, however, were full of splendid trees: oaks, pines, sassafras, juniper, birch, holly, vines, ash and walnut, and we returned to the *Mayflower* with a boatload of juniper. We purposely chose juniper because it burnt easily and also gave out a sweet aromatic fragrance reminiscent of incense, and this was especially appreciated after all the noisome smells we had endured aboard ship for so long.

Next day was the Sabbath, which was spent in prayer and thanksgiving. Pilgrims and Strangers alike fell on their knees and thanked God for bringing them safely to this new land, and I envied their unflinching trust that God would preserve them from all harm. The amazing courage of this brave little company never once failed them, yet to me, utterly devoid of their faith, the future appeared bleak indeed. The district we had come to was wild and desolate beyond belief.

Winter would soon be upon us, and we were hundreds of miles from the nearest settlement. My dreams of a land full of opportunity and promise had almost vanished, yet in a strange way the Pilgrims' unswerving optimism kept up my spirits.

On the following day, the 13th of November, the women went ashore to wash all their dirty clothes — a much needed exercise after the long sea journey. While they scrubbed, pummelled and rinsed, the children romped about, shouting and playing noisily, delighted to be away from the restricted space aboard ship. A shallop that had been stowed away between decks was now brought out and beached for repairs. We had hoped to use her for cruising about the coast in search of a more suitable site in which to form a colony, but she had been much damaged by the storms and was unseaworthy. So several of us under the direction of the ship's carpenter went to work on her, while the rest of the men combed the beach for shellfish. Before long they found an abundance of clams, quahogs, cherrystones and mussels, and we made a great feast of them, the first fresh food we had eaten for many weeks. Unhappily, the mussels, which I suspect had not been properly prepared, made us all very sick. But by great good fortune we soon recovered.

Two days later, when it became apparent that repairs to the shallop would take much longer than expected, it was felt we must find somewhere to live as quickly as possible. This decision was made more urgent by the attitude of the officers and men of the *Mayflower*. They were threatening to dump all passengers and their belongings on to the beach and sail for home, if we did not find somewhere soon. They wanted to leave, they said, before all their provisions were consumed. So I called for sixteen volunteers to help me to fix upon a likely place. I insisted that every man carried musket and sword and wore a helmet and corselet. Army discipline had taught me to be always prepared for the worst, while at the same time hoping for the best. As I bade Rose goodbye, it was like her not to voice her fears for my safety. Yet I knew her well enough to realise she was eaten up with anxiety and I tried to hearten her. I reminded her that I was a soldier, trained to take the utmost care of myself and my men, and that I was sure I would return safely. Finally, I think I convinced her, for she was soon talking happily of the home we would make together once we had found a suitable location.

So off we set again, walking in single file along the beach. After we had covered about a mile, we saw approaching us in the distance six Indians and a dog. They seemed harmless enough, for as soon as they spotted us they ran like frightened deer towards the woods. In vain I called to them, and made friendly gestures. I tried to make them understand we meant no harm and merely wanted to talk to them. We followed them for ten miles or more without success, and at length night fell and we had to camp until morning.

At dawn we set off after them again. It would have been a great help if we could have made friends with them. They would perhaps have sold us some of the seed corn which we so badly needed, and also have helped us to find some useful land to occupy and cultivate. Unfortunately, we lost their tracks in the woods and had

82

to abandon the chase altogether. I was vexed when I saw how much our chain armour had been damaged by the sturdy prickly shrubs through which we had pushed our way, and with nothing at all to show for it besides. To add to our difficulties, we had brought very little with us to eat or drink, except a few ships biscuits and some *aqua vitae*. Consequently, we were all parched with thirst, and there was nothing but dry land around us.

Yet I was determined not to return to the ship until I found something good to report. So, leaving the others, I went off to explore and, after prowling around for some time, I noticed a fall in the land, and had an idea that this would lead to a valley where there might be water. I ordered the men forward, and sure enough from the summit of a hill we saw a lake of pure fresh water down below. We were so thirsty that it tasted better than wine, and put new life into us. Close by the lake, there was land that had obviously once grown corn, and nearby we found several curious Indian graves covered with sand, old mats and wooden vessels. We dug down about a foot or so into one of them, and turned up a bow and some arrows that crumbled at a touch. No doubt they had belonged to a long dead warrior who lay buried below. A little further, we came upon the remains of a plank dwelling and a large kettle of European make which we took with us, probably the relics of a sea disaster.

On our way back to the ship, we saw more strange heaps of sand and, on digging again a few feet down into one of them, unearthed a large basket holding three or four bushels of corn. This was great good fortune. We hauled it up and filled the kettle with corn, resolving to repay the Indians if ever we came across them. As we marched on, we found the kettle very heavy to carry. It was slowing down our progress so, salvaging most of the corn into our pockets, we threw it away. Then, after spending another night in bivouac and a considerable time in further exploration, we arrived back at the ship. Everyone was overjoyed to see us and they were much encouraged by the news of our various discoveries, particularly when we showed them the corn.

During our absence, there had been an addition to our number, for Susanna White, one of the Pilgrims, had been delivered of a baby boy. They named him Peregrine, which was another apt choice, for I believe it means "a pilgrim".

CHAPTER TWENTY

Another ten days elapsed before the shallop, although not entirely restored, was fit enough to sail. Then thirty of us under the command of Captain Jones, skipper of the *Mayflower*, set off to explore the place more thoroughly. No sooner had we cast off than the weather broke, and we found ourselves beating up into a wild turbulent sea. Huge waves surged beneath the ship, causing it to lift and roll perilously. Then, to add to our discomfort, biting winds brought snow which covered the deck up to six inches deep. So, wearing ship, we made our way slowly and with great caution toward the mouth of the Panet river, which we had only hastily examined on our first trip.

Some of the company, impatient to land, waded ashore in icy water up to their hips and nearly froze to death. To make matters worse, the river entrance turned out to be both tidal and swampy, altogether too cramped for a ship as large as the *Mayflower* to pass through, although good enough for small boats to navigate. In spite of our disappointment, we edged the shallop into the harbour, disembarked and made straight for the meadow we had named Cornhill after finding corn there on our first expedition. The ground was now covered with snow, but we soon located the sand heap under which we had left the residue. The surface was now frozen hard but we were able, with our cutlasses and short swords, to uncover the large basket again and empty it of the remaining corn. We then dug into several similar heaps of snow-covered sand and unearthed more corn, amounting in all to about ten bushels, which we loaded into the shallop.

On looking back, I realise how lucky we were in this find, for I cannot imagine how we could possibly have survived without it. At the same time, I was sorry to deprive the Indians of their hidden store, for they must have needed it almost as much as we did. During the course of further digging, we came across several graves containing skeletons which, after removing sundry items, i.e. a knife, a few bowls, trays, a pack needle, trinkets and a few strings of white beads, we smoothed over again respectfully. Continuing our exploration, we came across some abandoned Indian round huts, from which we took away some earthen pots, wooden trays and fibre baskets, but we saw no people. They had evidently gone into hiding until they could ascertain whether or not we were friendly.

When we arrived back at the *Mayflower* and reported our findings, straightaway great arguments arose. Many of the company were all for settling immediately at Cornhill, pointing out its many advantages. The land was fertile and easy to defend. Also, being near at hand, it would save the task of further exploration during this time of inclement weather. While acknowledging the harbour to be poor, they still felt it to be capable of providing a safe enough anchorage. In addition, it gave promise of good fishing, for we had already sighted a few whales in the vicinity. However, others were against settling there. For one thing, they were not happy about the inadequate water supply which was wholly dependent on fresh water ponds, which could easily dry up in summer. Then a suggestion was put forward that we explore the far side of Cape Ann where the harbour was good and the fishing by all acounts excellent. And so the arguments went on and on, but it was quite by chance that the idea of settling at Cornhill was finally discarded.

One of the mates, Robert Coffin, was familiar with these waters and spoke of a good harbour, with a navigable river, directly across the bay. "Thievish Harbour" he called it because of an incident, involving a stolen harpoon, when he and some others had fished there some time before. So, on the strength of his report, twenty-eight of us, with Coffin at the tiller, set off again in the shallop to test its accuracy, and to inspect the surrounding countryside. Unhappily, the weather had not improved: if anything it had grown worse. A stiff breeze was blowing as we pulled away, and it was so cold that the spray, surging across the boat, cut like a knife and froze on our clothes until they were like coats of iron. Two of the men fainted with the cold but the rest of us held grimly on to our course and, sailing past Cornhill, rounded a sandy point into a sheltered bay, then made for the shore. We spent the night there around a blazing fire in the middle of a barricade of boughs and logs. Sentinels were placed on guard but we were not disturbed, even though we could see smoke rising from Indian fires some little distance away.

In the morning we split up into two companies, one to sail along the coast and the other to explore inland. We met again at night, and once more camped around a fire in a sheltered nook, with sentinels keeping watch as before. Early in the morning, before daybreak, some of the men took their arms down to the boat to protect them from the damp weather. This was against my advice for I believed it to be dangerous to be unarmed at this time.

I was soon to be proved right for, on their return to camp and just as dawn was breaking, a strange hoarse cry was heard. The sentinels gave the alarm, and their cry of "Indians, Indians" alerted all of us that were still sleeping. We were soon on our feet and it was fortunate that I and another man had kept our flintlocks by us, for those that had taken their muskets to the boat had to run back for them and, in no time at all, arrows came flying thick and fast amongst us. We let fly two shots at random: then I insisted on holding fire until the enemy drew closer. Still the arrows whistled and flew on all sides, only narrowly missing us, as the Indians crept stealthily forward. At intervals they repeated their wild war whoops, and it was a most eerie and unnerving sound to hear in the grey half-light of dawn.

As soon as they came near enough, I gave the order to fire a volley and they quickly dispersed. However, to my surprise, one of their number, a great sturdy fellow, decided to stay his ground. Hiding behind a tree, seemingly unafraid of our bullets, he sent down arrow after arrow in our direction. Then finally, after several shots had failed to dislodge him, I took aim at a portion of his anatomy that was sticking out from his hiding place. The shot was most effective but not in the way I had intended, for it shattered the bark of the tree into splinters which flew about his ears. Shrieking madly, he turned and ran to join his companions. We went after them and shot a piece or two to make sure they were still in retreat before returning to the boat. We took a number of their arrows with us, some handsomely finished with brass heads, others decorated with harts' horn and eagles' claws, flushed with triumph at the success of this first encounter with the Indians.

But "Pride", as the saying has it, "goes before a fall" and everything now began to work against us. High winds that had been blowing incessantly off the land now increased to gale force, and we were engulfed in yet another violent snow storm. The mast broke in three pieces and we lost a sail. Huge seas towered around the boat, lifted her up, pitched her forward and swung her about in every direction, until it was a fight to hold her. It was then, to our dismay, that Coffin realised that he had made a mistake and had never been in these waters before. He was gazing at the rough seas around us with troubled eyes as he confessed his blunder, and it seemed all too certain that we would be wrecked for we were in dire trouble. Then, just at that moment, the steersman shouted "Put about and row like fury, for there is a sound before us."

That was the miraculous turning point of our horrific journey as, bending to our task and rowing with all our strength, we drew into quieter waters under the lee of a dark strip of land. The danger was past but I could not help feeling horror-stricken at the thought of what might have happened had we not found shelter quickly. Darkness was falling and at first we decided to stay aboard until morning light, but later we were so cold and wet that instead we went ashore and, with some difficulty, lit a fire, which was a great comfort to our aching bones.

In the morning we discovered we had landed on an island and it was so peaceful and free from Indians that we stayed there for a couple of days to rest awhile, dry out our clothes and clean our weapons. We named the place Clark's Island after the mate of the *Mayflower*, then, as the third day dawned fine and calm, we sailed the shallop neatly into a wide harbour nearby and arrived at the place we were to call New Plymouth. It lay behind a great crag which we named Plymouth Rock, thus commemorating the port in England from which we had sailed.

We wasted no time in going ashore to make a survey of the land, for we had so little time and so much to evaluate. All the same I speedily came to the conclusion that, although not altogether ideal, it was by far the most habitable place we had yet come across. There were cornfields, little running brooks and wooded hills. Also we found many varieties of herbs and berries growing in profusion, and there was any amount of sand, gravel and fine clay for building purposes. From the upper part of the harbour we cruised along a large tidal inlet for several miles, and named it "Jones River" after the Master of the *Mayflower* who had, so patiently, sailed us about in search of a permanent resting place, when all he wanted really was to get back to England as soon as possible.

Within a week we returned to the *Mayflower* to report enthusiastically on our favourable discoveries, only to find everyone sad and downcast for, on the day after our departure, young Dorothy Bradford had fallen overboard and drowned while the boat was lying quietly at anchor. The curious circumstances of her death were puzzling. Her grief-stricken husband went about solemn and quiet, his face dark with misery, and to my knowledge never mentioned her name again. I and many others were of the opinion she had taken her own life, and I was confirmed in this belief when Rose mentioned that the poor woman had been withdrawn and depressed ever since leaving England and her little boy.

An air of melancholy pervaded the ship, but now a decision had to be made quickly regarding a settlement for the weather was worsening. A meeting was called and everyone gave their opinions and suggestions as to our next move, but eventually, after many arguments and weighing up of pros and cons, it was decided to take my advice and establish a colony at New Plymouth. Accordingly, a day or two later, we cast off again and sailed along with the *Mayflower* back across the bay, dropping anchor just outside the harbour. To be on the safe side in this severe winter weather, everyone was kept on board until we had built some sort of shelter. The *Mayflower*, owing to the shallowness of the harbour, was forced to be some distance away. So, taking twenty men with me in the shallop, I went ashore to clear the ground in preparation for the building of a common house. But now gale succeeded gale and caught us out in the open before we had time to build anything at all. The *Mayflower*, dragging her anchor, was being battered by huge waves that threatened at times to engulf her, and she jumped and swung about incessantly. One unfortunate woman, Mary Allen, was brought to bed at the very height of the storm and delivered of a son but, as was to be expected, he was unfortunately dead born.

Owing to the severity of the weather it was not until some time later, Christmas Day to be exact, that work really got under way. The Pilgrims did not recognise Christmas – they declared it a heathen festival, a relic of Pagan rites. So, during a lull in the storm, all able-bodied men came willingly ashore to fell timber and to saw and carry wood for our houses. First of all, a site was chosen and foundations laid for the Common House. But then another squall engulfed us and blew with even greater violence. I had never before experienced such mighty gusts of wind, and the delays to our work were maddening. Each night it rained hard, then froze during the day: therefore we could seldom work more than half a week at a time. In addition, as the *Mayflower* was lying a mile and a half off shore, much valuable time was lost in rowing to and fro.

Yet, in spite of these setbacks, New Plymouth gradually began to take shape. The main street of the town was laid out stretching along several hundred yards to the foot of a steep escarpment which we named Fort Hill. There, single handed, I built a wooden platform, strong enough to carry a cannon, for I judged it an excellent position from which to guard the town against possible marauding Indians. This main street was intersected by a twisty rough road, which led to a

87

little brook bordered on one side by rich grassy pastureland. On this place we made our first gardens, planting them with turnips, cabbage, parsnip and other seeds brought from England. Then, after completing the Common House, we built several temporary dwellings and, in order to provide living quarters more quickly for everyone, single men were asked to join a family for the time being.

The amount of land allocated to each household depended upon its size, so all heads of households were required to draw lots to determine which site each would occupy. And I must put it on record that at no time was there any scrambling to grab the best, no fraud or violence and no running after private gain. In spite of their bigotry and argumentative dispositions, I was forced to admire these Pilgrims, for they proved themselves to be a well-ordered, and caring, Christian community, all willing to pull together for the common good.

Occasionally, while at work in the clearing, we saw columns of smoke in the distance, but otherwise no sign of any human beings whatsoever. This puzzled me a little so, taking a few men with me, I went to investigate. But all we found were a few abandoned huts and an all-pervading ominous silence.

A few weeks later, when the fierce storms had abated somewhat, all the *Mayflower* company came ashore for the first time, but only for a short period, in order to attend a religious service organised by Ruling Elder Brewster. Everyone crowded into the Common House, and it was wonderful to have Rose beside me again, and to hear her sweet voice joining in the Pilgrims' psalms of thanksgiving to God for all His benefits. Before she returned with the others to the *Mayflower*, I took her to see the few small cottages we had built of wattle and daub, then we walked over to the plot allotted to me. It was situated at the foot of Fort Hill, so that I could get quickly to my post in time of danger. I had already laid the foundations of our house, and she was delighted at the prospect of soon being able to settle down and "strike roots" as she put it. She looked at me with a sudden smile as we stood there. "How wonderful to have a home of our own again" she said. She was radiant with happiness and I had never seen her look lovelier. But it was not until three months later that it was considered wise for everyone to come ashore for good.

Then, realistic as I had always been regarding the difficulties facing us, I now believed the worst of our trials to be over, sure that all we now had to do was to work hard and keep our wits about us in order to establish a flourishing colony. But I was terribly wrong for, because of the long delay in finding warm and adequate shelter during this dreadful winter, nearly everyone fell victim to a general sickness that threatened to wipe us all out. Months of semi-starvation together with cramped and unsanitary quarters, and exposure to all kinds of weather, had lowered resistance to disease and many died. The Common House was converted into a hospital and packed tight with sick beds. Then, to add to our difficulties, one night a spark from a fire flew up into the thatch which quickly ignited. Fiery embers dropped into the room below and caused great alarm, for several barrels of gunpowder and charged muskets lay about the place. The sick jumped from their beds and carried these outside, so preventing the whole building from being blown to pieces. By great good fortune the roof timbers held, and the damage was soon repaired, but alas the sickness now assumed epidemic proportions and many more perished.

Death also struck hard amongst the crew of the *Mayflower*, carrying off half the sailors, three of the mates, the master gunner, the bosun and the cook. Some of these I felt in some degree deserved their fate: the bosun for instance continually scoffed at the sick passengers. Still worse, when Bradford was stricken with the sickness and pleaded for some beer, he mocked him and swore that, if he were his own father, he should have none. Captain Jones, on learning of his cruelty, intervened and ordered beer for all that had need of it, even if it left none for the homeward journey. Later, when the bosun himself caught the sickness, the Pilgrims nursed him so carefully after he had been deserted by his boon companions that he repented and acknowledged his wickedness, but alas too late. On his deathbed he confessed: "You, I now see, show your love to all, like Christians should, but we let one another die like dogs."

Whole families amongst the Pilgrims were wiped out and only six or seven, including Rose and myself, were strong enough to get about to look after the rest. Accordingly, we worked night and day doing all we possibly could to mitigate their suffering. We fetched wood, lit fires, cooked meals and washed and dressed them – in short performed all the necessary, and sometimes loathsome, duties which so urgently needed to be done for all these desperately ill people, and I had never worked so hard in all my life. Rose went about her duties tirelessly. The invalids would hold out their hands to her and beg her to stay with them, and she sat at the bedsides of the dying, sometimes all night through. But in the end her physical make-up was unable to stand the strain, and hard work, together with lost sleep, began to take its toll.

One night as we were returning home after a bout of duty, I noticed with a sense of foreboding that she was heavy eyed and flushed. My heart sank and I was frightened. I asked her if she felt unwell. "I have a slight cold" she said: "nothing at all to worry about". But, as she spoke, she shivered and I felt her hand, which she had tucked in the crook of my arm, tremble. I stared at her in dismay, for I felt in my bones that something was seriously wrong.

Later, as we sat to our supper, I could quite plainly see that she was unwell. Suddenly she gave a gasp of pain, and fear clutched at my heart. I laid a hand on her forehead. It was burning and I had little doubt that she was yet another victim of the dreadful epidemic. I helped her to bed at once and went in search of the ship's doctor. When I returned with him, she had fallen into an uneasy sleep, but he confirmed my fears and said that she was by now critically ill. I did not go to bed that night, but sat watching my darling little wife as she lay there so still, her face unusually flushed, her breathing shallow and quick. There were beads of sweat on her forehead and now and then she gave a painful little cough. In the early hours she became delirious, muttering unintelligibly from time to time, then crying out for her mother and Barbara. Before dawn she awoke and became lucid again. She reached out and took my hand. "I am dying, Myles," she said, "but I am not afraid for I know that death is not the end but just another beginning."

Horror-stricken and too overcome with dread to reply, I shook my head — unable to accept that she was dying. "I wish you had my faith too, my darling," she went on, "for I love you so much and you have made me supremely happy during the whole time we have been together." Then, after a poignant silence during which I stroked her cheek while tears rained down my face, she said faintly "Please grieve for me a little, my dear." Whereupon, her eyes gradually became glazed and unseeing and I knew that my precious little wife had left me forever.

CHAPTER TWENTY-ONE

With unutterable sadness we buried her in the new graveyard called Colehill, where nearly half of our company now lay. The appalling shock of her death left me crushed with misery. I began to realise to the full just how much warmth and cheerfulness Rose had brought into my life, for now my days were empty and meaningless without her. Most of all, I was bowed down with remorse for having brought her across the ocean to perish in this dreary wilderness, where disease, privation and death prevailed. I went about for weeks in a kind of limbo, not caring whether I lived or died, seeing long, arid years ahead of me devoid of all joy. I carried on nursing the sick to the best of my ability although it was not easy, for melancholy afflicted me like a disease, and even the smallest task made me profoundly weary.

One bitterly cold night, after returning home from a spell of duty, I was sitting warming myself before a small fire of logs, feeling as usual sad, and very tired, when there came a knock on the door. Outside stood Edward Winslow, one of the Pilgrims whose wife, Elizabeth, had died the previous week. "I was passing and saw your light" he said in a low voice, almost a whisper. "May I come in for a while?"

"Certainly" I said, and taking his arm drew him into the room. I was truly glad to see him, for all at once I had a wild craving for sympathy, for the company of another human being.

He came and sat with me by the fire, a tall fine-looking man, powerfully built with strong features and dark hair peppered with grey. To-night his face was deadly pale and showing signs of great strain. For a few moments there was silence between us. Several times he looked at me anxiously, then away again as if about to speak, yet not knowing how to begin. At last he leaned forward and gazed earnestly into my eyes. "We two are companions in distress" he said gently. Then, choosing his words carefully, he went on: "We have both lost the other half of ourselves, and it hurts almost beyond endurance. Is that not so?"

I nodded, but felt too heartbroken to speak.

He bent his head and stared down at his feet that I might not too clearly see the tears that were coursing down his cheeks, and I realised that here was a man every bit as lonely and bereft as I was.

We sat quietly together for a time, in some strange way drawing comfort from our mutual anguish. After a time he lifted his head and, looking beyond me into the fire, began to talk of his wife. He went back over the years to the day they had just met, then to their courtship and marriage, and his face was alight with pride as he told me of her great qualities, of her wisdom and loving kindness. "I am so grateful to have had such a splendid companion, and it is a wonderful consolation to know we shall meet again in heaven."

Here I broke in: "Then I must say you are more fortunate in your solace than I am. For I believe neither in God nor His heaven. Tell me", I said, "how you can possibly reconcile your belief in a kind heavenly Father with the suffering He permits His children to endure?"

Edward Winslow smiled and turned on me a look of infinite forbearance: "Because", he said gently, "all true Christians know that Heaven is their final goal, and many go on before. We should be glad for them and try not to grieve unduly, as those without hope in the world. The body dies but the spirit lives on, and the parting is only for so short a time in the light of eternity."

I gazed on him in wonderment, for here was a man as heartbroken as myself yet not in despair. He did not worry about the profound questions of life and death, but trusted in God in a simple, childlike way, and, listening to him, I was impressed by the logic of his argument. For the first time I began to wonder whether, if after all, there was something in the Christian doctrine. Before leaving, he grasped both my hands in his and, full of the assurance of one brought up in the Pilgrims' Faith, his voice resonant and his eyes gleaming with fervour, he said "I tell you this, my friend. I do not grieve for any in their dying except for those that die without faith in the love of God. Believe me, God has a reason for everything. There are no untimely deaths, and in time we shall both see a pattern emerge – a meaning for it all".

The only response I felt able to make at that moment was to thank him for his visit and to beg him to come again soon. "It has been a great comfort to have someone to talk to" I said.

He smiled but, without another word, turned abruptly and hurried away into the cold, dark night.

I went to bed late that night but not to sleep. Hour after hour I lay there in the dark, weighed down with misery. I thought of Winslow and envied him his faith in the goodness and wisdom of God; and, although I did not want God, I craved for consolation and relief from suffering. At last, baffled and perplexed, I found myself praying for the first time in many years. "Oh God", I groaned, "if you exist, please help me for I am at the end of my tether." Soon after I fell into a sound sleep, and it was mid-morning before I awoke.

That evening Edward Winslow called on me again. He did not refer to our previous conversation but came with a message from Governor Carver, asking me to attend a General Meeting. This was to be held in the Common House, which was no longer full of sick beds, for all had recovered sufficiently to be looked after in their own homes. Winslow and I walked down the road to the meeting, talking easily together and, although I was still feeling depressed, it was a comfort to have him at my side. In his own quiet way, he was immensely sincere and steadfast, and from that day sprang a friendship that has grown and strengthened through the years right up to the present time.

When we arrived at the Common House, we found all the male members of the community already assembled there, and I was pleased to see they had obeyed my instructions to carry their muskets with them at all times, in case of trouble with the Indians. A few minutes later, Governor Carver trod slowly in and gathered us around him in a circle. He was a man of strong and active presence, massively built with a big hook of a nose and a firm chin, yet at the same time he was surprisingly unassuming in manner.

Stern-faced and solemn, he told us that, on several occasions lately, Indians had been seen skulking around on the edge of the town, and had run off into the surrounding woods when they were recognised. But, in the early hours of the morning, they had crept into the town and stolen a quantity of much needed workmen's tools. He feared they had somehow discovered that our numbers were greatly depleted, and might be about to chance their luck in a sudden foray – this in spite of the fact that all our dead had been buried at night and the graves smoothed over and planted with corn to hide our losses from them. Consequently, he proposed that our defence should be more properly organised, so that each man would know exactly what to do in time of danger.

By popular vote, the company chose me to be Captain General and gave me authority of command in all their affairs. This was a post as important in the Council of State as the Governor himself and I could not help feeling proud that these people had shown such confidence in my ability to protect them. Then, for more than an hour we discussed tactics and strategy, and had almost consolidated our plans for countering an attack when an Indian brave was spotted striding boldly down the main street of the town. He would have walked straight into the Common House had not the sentries prevented him, and sounded out a warning. We ran out from the meeting, muskets at the ready, but, as we approached him, we were astonished to hear him cry out in good English "Welcome Englishmen, Welcome English. I am Samoset, chief of the tribe of Abnaki."

We clustered around him, a little warily at first, but soon decided the fellow was friendly enough and took him into the Common House for interrogation. He bowed and smiled, seemingly quite willing, even pleased, to answer all our questions, and was throughout most affable and courteous. He told us he had learned to speak our tongue while working with some English fishermen from higher up the coast, and proceeded to give us valuable information about the surrounding Indian tribes and the general condition of the countryside. It appeared there had once been an Indian village here at Plymouth called Pantuxet, but all the former inhabitants had died during a great plague, which by the symptoms he described I judged to be smallpox. This then solved the mystery of the abandoned cornfields, and the absence of Indians in the neighbourhood.

The most powerful chief in the district was, he told us, Massasoit, head of the Wampanoag tribe who lived about forty miles south-west of Plymouth. They exercised dominion over every tribe in the south-eastern corner of New England, including those in Cape Cod called the Nauset. It was this tribe, he said, that had fallen upon our exploring party near the elbow of the Cape and had been routed in confusion. It was quite late when we finished questioning him, so he spent the night at the house of Stephen Hopkins, one of our leading members.

Next morning we presented him with a knife, a bracelet and a ring, as a gesture of goodwill, and he swaggered off into the distance well pleased with these gifts. A few days later, however, he turned up again, accompanied by five more braves, each carrying a deerskin and several beaverskins, which they laid at the door of the Common House. We were particularly pleased with the beaver skins for beaver was a valuable fur, and brought high prices in England. So we prevailed upon Samoset to send them back for more, telling him we were willing to barter generously for skins like these. For, if only we could get hold of them in any quantity, we would soon be able to pay off our debt to the sponsoring company. Unfortunately for us, they did not return, and four days later Samoset went off to find them. After a couple of days, he came back without the braves but with a friend called Sqanto who, to our amazement, also spoke good English.

He told us a strange tale of how he had been kidnapped twice – once by an English captain who had carried him away to Plymouth in England, from whom, after a year or two, he was able to escape and had, by some means, found his way back home. He was taken a second time while fishing, and shipped off with twenty of his companions to Spain, where they were sold as slaves. Escaping again, he had actually joined the crew of a ship bound for the Massachusets coast only to find all his people had perished in the great plague. When he learned that he was the only surviving member of the Pantuxet tribe, he went to Massasoit at Sowams, and the great chief took him in. When he had finished his long story, he gave us the startling news that Massasoit wished for a meeting with us, and was even now on his way, accompanied by his brother Quadiquina and a large number of braves.

Before long the great chief and his retinue arrived and stood, grouped together and strangely silent, on the summit of Strawberry Hill overlooking the town. They were a truly awesome sight as they stood there, absolutely motionless, observing us from the hill-top. Massasoit, a great lusty fellow, had a deerskin fastened over one shoulder and a great chain of white bone beads about his neck. The muscles of his huge bare arms stood out like cords and gleamed in the sunshine. Sixty fierce-looking braves surrounded him, all heavily painted in black, red, yellow and white stripes, each one decorated with crosses and many other ornaments. Altogether, there were more than three times the number of men we could muster and, as I looked them over, I was for a moment filled with consternation. But then, as quickly as possible, I assembled my men and fitted them up with as much armour and steel as I could gather together, and in the event contrived to put up a quite formidable array. We stood waiting at the foot of the hill in orthodox military formation as Samoset and Squanto took the Indians a message of welcome.

They came back with an invitation from Massasoit for the Pilgrim leaders to come over to them for a pow-wow. This the leaders flatly refused to consider, and things were at a rather dangerous impasse when Winslow asked, and obtained permission, to act as intermediary. He took Samoset with him as interpreter and also brought them several gifts – a knife for Quadequina and a jewel to hang in his ear: a pair of knives for the chief as well as a jewelled copper chain, biscuits, butter and a jar of *aqua vitae*. In the end, he arranged that he would stay with Quadequina as hostage while Massasoit came to pay his respects to Governor Carver. So, leaving behind their bows and arrows, twenty of his finest warriors accompanied him as, with great grandeur, he slowly descended the hill to be saluted by my men, who looked as martial and awe-inspiring as possible.

Massasoit stood three or four heads taller than I but, as I went forward to greet him, I was determined to show no fear. So, placing myself boldly at his right hand, with my men marching behind me, I escorted him and his men down the main street through a line of women and children, all agape with curiosity. I led him to an almost completed house, which had been hastily furnished for the occasion with a green rug and a few cushions. He had no sooner settled himself when, with a loud blaring of drums, Governor Carver appeared. The big chief rose and kissed his hand, and for a moment or two both men eyed one another cautiously. Then Governor Carver called for a pot of hard liquor and, with a great deal of formality, they drank to each other's health.

When at last we did get down to serious talk, we found there were many things to discuss. Massasoit, solemn and dignified, told us plainly why they felt bitter towards the English, and why they wished to drive us away. For years, he said, English captains had continually robbed them, kidnapped their young men and killed many of their people with "firesticks". He also suspected, not, I might add, without good reason, that English ships had brought the terrible plague to their land. As he spoke, his eyes flashed with fury and the atmosphere grew tense, but Squanto and Samoset acted as mediators.

They explained that we wished to live at peace with the Indians, and to trade with them honestly. Eventually, we convinced Massasoit of our good intentions, and in the end negotiated a peace treaty which gave satisfaction to both sides. We had one great advantage in that the Massasoits were frequently at war with their neighbours, the Narraganset, and Squanto used this knowledge to devise an excellent code of conduct. This provided that the Indians gave back the stolen tools and we in turn would pay for the corn we had taken. Each group undertook to punish any one of their people who might offend the other. Neither would go to the other with weapons in their hands and, if a third group attacked either side, the other would come to their aid. It was a fair treaty and I for one was well satisfied with the day's work.

CHAPTER TWENTY-TWO

With everything happening so quickly and so much to organise, I had little time to brood, and at length I felt composed enough to write two necessary letters. One to Barbara and the other to George and Kitty, telling them my sad news. It was a task I had been dreading, and I performed it with a heavy heart, but it had to be done before the *Mayflower* left for England as it could be many months before another ship sailed into the harbour. I entrusted the letters to Captain Jones, who undertook their safe delivery. Then, on a soft sunny morning in early April, at last the *Mayflower* sailed away for home. Everyone gathered at the quayside as she drew away, and we watched her go with deep misgivings.

Now we were entirely on our own as a community, cut off from all outside help. Also it worried us that we had sent her back with an empty hold, for after the past long hard months we had been unable to spare any cargo at all, and we were still heavily in debt to the sponsoring merchants in London.

About a week after the *Mayflower* left us, we suffered a terrible calamity, for John Carver died suddenly while planting corn in the fields. He was greatly lamented, having won general respect for his wise and kindly leadership. Then, after a suitable time, William Bradford was elected Governor in his place, and this was an excellent choice for he was by far the cleverest and most far-sighted man of us all.

Meanwhile, Samoset left us to return to his tribal homeland, but Squanto was content to stay and, to the intense gratification of the Pilgrims, he accepted their Faith, joined the Christian community and worshipped with them regularly. He proved to be a great asset to us for, with the advance of spring, he worked hard and willingly in the fields from dawn until sunset. He also made himself invaluable by teaching us many curious techniques: how to plant corn four kernels to the hillock in time-honoured Indian fashion and how to use the fish called Alwife, which abounded in the bay, along with herring from the brook as manure for the corn. This, placed in the earth along with the seed, produced abundant crops far exceeding our wildest dreams. He also taught us an easy method of tapping maple trees for their sweet syrup, and many ingenious ways of trapping deer and game, so all in all I do not know how we could have managed so well without him.

With all this farming lore, together with the added benefit of glorious weather, summer brought us great good fortune. Corn ripened in the fields, grapes grew warm in the sun and we were able to trade with the Indians for a good supply of beaver skins. Then, because this first autumn in New England, so mellow and beautiful, had brought us such an abundant harvest, Governor Bradford thought it fitting to inaugurate a day of general thanksgiving. So, on a suitable day in October with the sun shining brightly in a cloudless sky, he sent Squanto with an invitation to Massasoit and some of his braves to join us in the feast.

Four of our men were delegated to shoot waterfowl, and they returned with enough ducks, geese and wild turkeys to keep the whole company for a week. Even so an embarrassing situation arose when Massasoit arrived bringing with him upwards of ninety hungry braves for, in spite of all our preparations, we knew we were unable to feed such a large number. Massasoit must have noticed our concern, for he immediately sent a few of his men off into the forest and it was not long before they returned bringing many fine deer as their contribution to the feast. In the end we sat down to goose and venison, lobster by the score, ell pie and corn bread with fresh herbs, wild plums and berries, served together with white and red wine. The Indians enjoyed themselves so much that they stayed with us for three days, and even then left with great reluctance.

It was round about this time that one of the Pilgrims, John Alden, was sent by Governor Bradford to share my house and help me build up our defences. He was a shy young fellow, tall, fair-skinned and handsome, a cooper by trade but able to turn his hand to most things. He was particularly helpful in preparing wood for stockades and erecting temporary shelters for tools and other equipment, and, possessing great bodily strength, he gave me great assistance in the building of a pallisade round our little town. We found such a protection necessary for, although we had a good relationship with Massasoit, the Narrangasetts were still hostile. Their chief, Canonicus, had recently sent to Governor Bradford a sheaf of arrows wrapped in a large snakeskin which, Squanto assured us, was a challenge to battle. Without more ado, Bradford returned the snakeskin stuffed with bullets and a message to the effect that we were well prepared for war if that was their wish. This apparently scared them to death, as we heard no more from them for some considerable time, and we were left to establish our colony in peace and quiet.

We were able now to concentrate on finding more supplies of beaver. Also, from time to time, I went out in the shallop accompanied by Squanto and had many good catches of cod. This was a most useful addition to our diet, since there was no sign of fresh supplies of food from England as had been promised. So, one way and another, the township gradually grew strong and prosperous, for we all lived together peacefully, each one working for the good of the community.

I had by now resigned myself to a fairly lonely life, but John Alden proved to be pleasant company, and his presence in the house made life more bearable. For long months nothing seemed to change. Then one day a tall white sail was sighted off Cape Cod making for the harbour. It was the fifty-five ton *Fortune*, which had sailed from London four months earlier. On board were 35 men, women and children, most of them our old friends from Leyden, and there were many joyful reunions. Alas they brought no food with them, but a severe reprimand from the merchant sponsors for sending no lading in the hold of the *Mayflower*. But the Captain also had a quantity of letters for us, two of which were for me. I opened that from George and Kitty first, and read it with a sinking heart, for their expressions of love and sympathy brought me to the edge of tears, and a rush of longing to see them and talk to them again. Then I opened the letter from Barbara, and suddenly the whole course of my life changed.

"Dear Myles", she wrote,

"I am heartbroken to learn that our darling Rose has died. I loved her so dearly, my gentle, good little sister, and it is hard to realise I will never see her again in this life. I grieve for you too, my dear, in your great sorrow, and I have some idea of how you must be suffering, inasmuch as I have also been cruelly bereaved, for Thomas Cleator, whom I was to marry shortly after you left, died, as you know, when he was gored by a bull while working on the home farm. He was a dear, good man and his death, so terrible and painful, has left me unbearably lonely for more than ten years. Do you think, Myles, that it would help us both if I came to join you in your new country: perhaps we could comfort one another. You once told me you loved me, and I for my part have never ceased to love you. Perhaps you do not now want to marry me, but if you do, I will join you just as soon as I can take a passage.

Yours as ever,
Barbara."

As I read her letter, my heart leapt with joy. Frank and open as ever, she had written without mock modesty, straight from her honest heart. I knew, of course, that I loved her still and always had. It was in a different way from my love of Rose, deep and genuine though that had been. How curious, I thought, that I could love two women so dearly. Although never once during my marriage had I allowed myself to think of Barbara in any but a brotherly fashion, yet now I knew without a shadow of doubt that, deep within myself, I had always cared for her. I wrote at once to tell her all that was in my heart, and begged her to come to me as soon as possible. I gave my letter into the safe keeping of Captain Thomas Barton of the *Fortune* for urgent despatch, and for the rest of the day went about dazed with happiness.

CHAPTER TWENTY-THREE

In a curious sense I was now living in a different world, a world full of joy and delight. I told no-one of my plans to marry again: somehow I enjoyed keeping them to myself, a delicious secret to cherish in private. Furthermore, we were all kept too busy to have much time for confidences, for everyone was working hard to fill up the hold of the *Fortune*. We stuffed her chock-full of hardboard, timber, hardwood and good wainscotting, and with many hogheads of beaver and otter pelts as well. Altogether, this cargo was valued at £500, almost half the debt outstanding to the London merchants. This we hoped would put them in good humour and encourage them to send us more provisions, since we now had many more mouths to feed after the last influx of immigrants, and our food stocks were running perilously low.

Besides helping each day to load up the *Fortune*, I had also recently reorganised the army, dividing it into four parts, with a commander in charge of each company. Our position I felt to be precarious, surrounded as we were by several tribes of unfriendly Indians. So, as soon as the task of stowing the cargo was finished, I went to each member in turn to inform him I had arranged a general mobilisation. This was in order to give some information on the handling of arms, and also to test the men's acquaintance with their duties.

It was late afternoon when I arrived at Master Mullins' house, one of the Pilgrim leaders, my last port of call. I was tired and only stayed long enough to give him briefly my message. As I was leaving, his daughter, Priscilla, said she wanted a breath of fresh air before supper and would walk with me as far as my house. I had always been fond of Priscilla. I had watched her grow from a leggy, chirpy, little girl into a beautiful young woman, and there had always been a bond of sympathy between us. She was about nineteen years old, well built, with light brown hair, large green eyes, a round dimpled face and an engaging smile.

We walked along in silence for a moment or two, then she turned her face towards me and said, shyly, "You are looking much happier these days, Captain Myles, and I am glad. I was afraid you were going to be miserable for the rest of your life." I gazed at her doubtfully, not wanting to share my secret. Then, in spite of myself, I began to unfold the whole story of Rose and Barbara, and let fall that Barbara was soon to join me. She listened gravely and, when I had finished speaking, she said "You are a very lucky man to have won the affections of two good women, both of whom you have cared for so deeply."

I was struck by something wistful and forlorn in her voice and said gently "You too will find happiness one day with a good man, Priscilla."

She shrugged her shoulders, then gave me a quick sideways glance. "I am already in love", she said, "and I feel sure my love is returned, but the young man in question has never once said so. He is so shy that I fear he never will." She spoke with sadness, and gave a great sigh that tugged at my heart.

"Who is he?" I asked.

"John Alden" she said. Then, looking straight at me and blushing to the roots of her hair, she went on "He calls for me when we attend the meetings, and always walks home with me afterwards, yet never once has he spoken a loving word, or even held my hand. I have given him every chance I can think of to encourage him to declare himself, but all to no avail – yet I am quite sure he is fond of me."

I stared at her incredulously. John had always seemed totally uninterested in the opposite sex, spending all his spare time in carving and woodwork, and I had come to the conclusion that he was that strange creature – a confirmed bachelor. Priscilla had turned her face away from me in obvious embarrassment but, in a little while, when she looked at me again, her eyes were troubled and full of tears. "I want to have a home and children of my own", she said in a tremulous whisper, "but I am certain that John will never come to the point of asking me to marry him."

For a while I said nothing. I was finding it a little difficult to put into words an idea that had just floated into my mind. I suppose most people happily in love are potential matchmakers, and I found I was no exception. Then, taking the bull by the horns, tentatively I put forward a proposition. I told her I would send John Alden over to her house that very night to ask her to marry me for, as I had been a widower for some time now, I felt he would not think it unseemly of me to want to marry again. Furthermore, I would explain to him that he would be able to plead my cause much better than I could for I had always been a soldier and, therefore, inordinately inept and awkward with womenfolk. "That done", I said, "I will leave the rest to your womanly intuition." I looked at her for agreement.

A delighted smile spread over her face. Then she threw her head back and laughed aloud. "Captain Myles", she said, "you are a great rogue but I think your plan might work." We shook hands conspiratorially as we reached my house, and I smiled to myself as I watched her turn and walk back home, head held high and humming a little tune to herself as she went.

That evening, after supper, I sat by the fire reading. John Alden was at the far end of the room, working on some oak beams he had found washed up on the shore, out of which he was fashioning some excellent shelves to hold our cooking utensils and various culinary articles. As he worked he was whistling tunelessly to himself through his teeth, completely absorbed in his work. I glanced over at him once or twice but found it difficult to broach the subject uppermost in my mind. At last I put my book down, cleared my throat and turned to face him.

"John," I said, "I have a great favour to ask you. It is difficult for me but I have no-one else to turn to." I was speaking with a solemn expression and John gazed

100

at me a little uneasily, yet underneath his natural kindness filled him with sympathy for my dilemma, whatever it was.

"I will do all in my power to help you" he said, but soon after, as I outlined my plan for him to ask Priscilla to marry me, his expression darkened. He heard me out, then, hesitating a little, he reminded me sharply that Priscilla was much younger than I, another generation in fact. "Have you any inkling that she would consent to be your wife?" he asked.

"No," I answered, "but it is high time she had a husband, and there are not many eligible suitors around."

His face was creased with anxiety, but I could see him making an effort to disguise his chagrin. There was a long silence between us, then suddenly he came to a decision. Looking straight at me, and in a most doleful tone, he said "I will do my best for you. I am not sure you have picked the right man for the task, but I will go immediately to see what can be done."

This reaction was exactly what I had hoped for. "Good fellow" I cried. "I wish you all the luck in the world."

He turned, and for a moment gave me a pained look, then went quickly, closing the door behind him.

In less than an hour he was back, bringing Priscilla with him. His whole expression was fiercely happy and her face radiant with joy. Then, slightly flushed, he came over and shook my hand. "Captain Myles," he said in a low voice, "when I left this house I was the most miserable man in all our town, and now I am the happiest. Thank you for showing me how much I loved Priscilla."

I turned to Priscilla, grinning all over my face: "I think I have earned the right to know exactly what transpired between you two."

She chuckled fondly, then described in detail John's miserable expression as he pleaded for me. "He extolled your virtues to the skies, enlarging on the fact that, as you had already proved yourself to be a good, fond husband, he was sure, in spite of your age, I would find you all I desired in life." She half turned and gave John a roguish look. "I let him go on and on and, when he had no more to say, I said quietly 'Why do you not speak for yourself, John?' Then I put my arms around him and kissed him. He held me tight and told me how much he loved me. Then he broke off to ask me how we would break the news to you. I told him your bride would soon be on the high seas, and that it had all been a ruse to bring him to the point of asking me to marry him."

Here I broke in: "She will make you an excellent wife, John," I said, "but do not think it was all due to me that you have come together. I am sure it would have come out all right in the end, but hope deferred was making Priscilla heartsick and this little push has only hurried matters along, and I am very happy for you both."

In a matter of weeks they were married and allocated a small house of their own, which John, with his great skills at woodwork, soon transformed into the most comfortable living quarters in the community.

Meanwhile, I had to force myself to await the arrival of Barbara with patience

101

but, before she arrived, there were many long and bitter disappointments to bear. To begin with the *Fortune*, by whom we had set such great store in bringing back good relations between the London merchants and ourselves, was captured by a French privateer and stripped of almost everything of any value, even taking the sheet anchor and some of her sail before allowing her to make her way up the Thames.

Then, to my great dismay, just when I needed all my health and strength I fell seriously ill of a fever, and it was some time before I was able to take command of the army again. Added to this, a poor harvest had left most of us hungry, distraught and irritable. So, as soon as I recovered, I sailed for the Cape in search of fish which were to be found there in great abundance. I had several good catches which were greatly appreciated, and was also able to purchase some much needed corn from an Indian tribe living on the coast. However, I found some of the tribes unfriendly, and for many months we had serious trouble from the Nauset, Commaquid, Manomet, and Ponet Indians, who time and again raided our township. In the end, I was forced to slay many, including Witunamat, a chief, for which I received much criticism, although to my mind I could, for the sake of protecting my fellow countrymen, do nothing less. "Oh", wrote John Robinson, "how happy a thing if you had converted some before you killed any." But for my part I think they deserved their fate. It was to be my men or them, and I chose the Indians. All that transpired has been set down by Governor Bradford and my case rests with him.

At this time, I suffered another worry when there were hints that the *Little James*, the vessel I expected to bring Barbara, had not been seen for some time, and I was mad with suspense. I felt sure that fate was about to deal me yet another bitter blow. Hope for her was almost dead when, many weeks overdue, she was sighted on the horizon making swiftly for land, and with the wind behind her and a fine spread of sail she was soon about to enter the harbour. A large crowd had gathered as she drew alongside, for many were waiting to greet old friends and relations from the community in Holland who had at last decided to join us here in America.

I find it difficult to describe my feelings as I stood at the end of the jetty and spotted Barbara leaning against the ship's rail, her eyes searching for me amongst the crowd. Although she had matured somewhat since I last saw her, she had lost none of her handsome good looks, and I felt very conscious of my own shortcomings in that direction. Small of stature as I have always been, my hair was now well sprinkled with grey, and my wrinkled face bore witness to the many vicissitudes I had suffered. I wondered sadly if Barbara would still find me acceptable as a husband. Soon she recognised me and waved with gusto. She was the first to disembark and ran straight into my outstretched arms. As I gazed into her steadfast eyes, she gave me a long loving look and I knew that all was well.

I had arranged for Governor Bradford to marry us as soon as Barbara arrived so, after settling with one of the sailors to deliver Barbara's luggage to my house, we went first of all to the Bradford's home where, in the presence of several of the elder brethren, we were joined together in wedlock.

In the meantime, Priscilla and John Alden had organised a wedding feast to which all the community was invited: a feast as usual of roast duck, clams and other shellfish, white bread, corn bread, wild plums and dried berries, washed down with wine made of the wild grape. It was all a great success, and the general atmosphere was of happiness and great goodwill towards Barbara and myself.

Later, as we walked home together, I was too overcome with emotion and happiness to speak much. Not so Barbara. She was all set to talk, and sailed on with the latest news of our friends in the Isle of Man. George and Kitty (who sent their fondest love) were now retired and living in a cottage on their son's farm at Sulby. Huan had married a local girl and had a son and daughter, and I was gratified to learn he had called the little boy "Standish" after me, although I dare bet that Kitty had something to do with that.

The Karrans were all well and happy and had a little family of two boys and a girl. Edward was still going strong and very active, which was wonderful news, but I was cut to the quick when Barbara told me of the painful and cruel death that both Father McAuley and Edmund Arrowsmith had suffered at the hands of religious fanatics.

Not surprisingly, my little mare Peggy had died, but I was on the edge of tears when I learned that, at Barbara's request, she had been buried at the far end of the meadow where she had spent her last years, and that a little headstone there bore the inscription "Peggy, dear friend and companion of Myles Standish of Ellanbane and New Plymouth".

Then Barbara let fall that Cousin William had gone through all his money. Furthermore, he was even now in the process of selling Ellanbane to cover his gambling debts, and I must admit it gave me some satisfaction to know he had benefited so little from his treachery.

CHAPTER TWENTY-FOUR

And now fifteen years have elapsed since Barbara and I were married. Wonderful years of love and fulfilment. We have a fine healthy family of four boys and a girl, and we are supremely content. In addition, I am happy to say that all has gone well with the whole community. Harvests have been good, we have paid all our debts to the London merchants and, in spite of many difficulties from the Indians and even from various white settlers along the coast, which we found even harder to bear, everyone here is well fed and prosperous.

During the past few years, several of us have moved across the Panet river to Ducksburrow, so named because of the great colonies of ducks settled there, and we have found the land rich, productive and easy to farm.

Meanwhile, another great happiness has come into my life, albeit rather late, for Barbara, always an earnest Christian, has persuaded me of the goodness of God, and His loving plan of salvation through His Son, Jesus Christ. And I must agree with her that all things really have worked together for good for both of us. Yet, although we are practising Christians, we have not joined the Pilgrim persuasion. For it is still my firm belief that all forms of organised religion are intolerant and arrogant, and the cause of much dissension and bloodshed in the world. We try as far as we can to follow the golden rule, which is hard enough to live out in all conscience, without the restricting shibboleths of any creed.

So all is set fair and we are full of love and loyalty for this new country that has given us so much, and yet we are often homesick for our native Island so far away, and hope against hope that some day we will be able to return, if only for a visit, to our own dear Ellan Vannin with its green hills by the sea.